CRESCENT CITY SIN

BOOK 2

THE CRESCENT CITY SERIES

NOLA NASH

RAMIREZ AND CLARK, LLC

PRAISE FOR NOLA NASH

Crescent City Sin is akin to drinking a potion bubbling with intriguing supernatural and mysterious twists! A powerful, supernatural escape to historic New Orleans! ~Ann Charles, USA Today Bestselling Author

Nola Nash delivers a powerhouse of a sequel to Crescent City Moon with her newest addition. Combine the dark under-belly of New Orleans with voodoo, a resurrected witch, true love, a nun and a mysterious stranger with a past that binds them all together and you have an enormously satisfying thriller that should not be missed! ~ Laura Kemp- award-winning author of The Lantern Creek Series

"Even in the grave, all is not lost." Edgar Allan Poe

Crescent City Sin
By

Nola Nash

CHAPTER

ONE

Things put underground in New Orleans don't often stay there. Even the darkest of buried things are pushed back up and into the light eventually. Nothing is truly immune to the pull of the surface. Even things that should be. Like bodies. And secrets.

Darkness can, if only briefly, hide a multitude of sins.

CHAPTER

TWO

Words floated like snowflakes through the mist of her mind. Darting and dancing in the wind. Familiar, yet foreign. She tried to grab onto one, to hold the word long enough to see what it was, the detail, the beauty. Reaching for it only pushed it farther away.

She didn't know what the words were or what they meant, but she knew she needed them more than anything else. Words so soft, earnest, and pure. Panic began to seize her as the words drifted away. Soft, earnest, and pure. She wanted to run. To chase them into the mist and snatch them from the swirling air. Her feet refused. Rooted her to the spot where she stood.

At least, she thought she stood. Was she standing? There was only mist, and white, and words. The words that were everything.

"Zéolie?" the mist asked. She blinked hard at it. Had she heard her name? Surely not. "Zéolie, can you hear me?" Nod. Recognition, but not understanding. "Good," the mist said. Haze gathered. Silvery and bright. Transparent became opaque. Opaque became solid. Beauty from nothing.

The mist smiled at her. Gentle and familiar, like family. Strong, but serene. A hand was extended. A hand was taken. Warm despite the icy whiteness. "I don't understand," Zéolie whispered. Her voice lost itself in the mist and words. Words. Still floating out of reach. Soft. Persistent.

Shaking her head, the mist said, "No, and I can't explain. Not yet. Not now." Another hand was extended. Another hand was taken. Warm.

"Why?" Zéolie asked. The question hung thickly.

Silver mist sighed. A whisper in a snow-coated forest. "It's not time."

"When?" The question begged an answer but was disappointed.

Words pulsed in the mist. Fervent. Impassioned. Pleading. Solid silver mist began to melt. Wavering. Unsure. Silver became gold. Cold became warmth. Glowing. Flickering. Fading.

"Camille?" Zéolie asked.

Golden mist nodded. Smiled. A tear fell. Silver. Shimmering. Hands were released. Whiteness faded to gray. Blackness settled. "*Vous n'êtes pas fini.* You aren't finished," the thinning mist said. Golden flickering in the blackness. A bell. Soft, tinkling, muffled. Words ceased. Quiet. Only the bell. Heaviness. Tightness. Heat. Smells. Wood, wax, and dust. The bell. Voices panicked. Pain blinded. Darkness enveloped. Darkness hid.

CHAPTER

THREE

Candlelight fluttered around the small convent sanctuary, glinting off candlesticks and statues. In a small chalice on the altar, crimson wine shimmered. A thin white wafer lay on the altar cloth, abandoned. To one side, a dark carved seat with a ramrod straight back was occupied by a slumped figure. Shoulders accustomed to carrying the city's souls sagged under a different weight. Aging white hands rested limply on black cloth. The rosary they once clutched tightly lay on the gleaming wood floor. Gray eyelashes sparkled with tears.

"Mother Micheaux?" a small voice said from the far end of the chapel.

The figure raised her eyes, but not her head. "Yes?"

"Sister Rosalie wanted to know if you would be blessing supper, or if you would like her to do it again?" the novice asked.

"Tell her I would be grateful if she would do the blessing." Eyes lowered, not waiting on a response.

"Yes, Mother," the girl said and left as quietly as she came.

Her eyes closed, willing words to come. Words to prayers she knew all her life. Prayers of blessing and thanks. Prayers of forgiveness and hope. The words were gone. Other words had taken their places. Words she couldn't utter in this holy place.

She stood. Her hand instinctively reached for the rosary on the floor and threaded it through the belt at her waist. It hung like a stone, heavy and lifeless, making her more conscious of the missing prayers.

Pushing the dead weight of it aside in her mind, she moved toward the side door of the sanctuary and put her hand on it. For a moment, she had the urge to go back to the altar and try again but knew it would do no good. The words were gone.

The dark figure of the mother superior passed through the door into a dimly lit corridor. It was deserted with all the sisters at dinner. Across the convent, there was the soft murmur of voices, the chink of forks on plates, and the gurgle of water being poured in cups. In the corridor, there was silence. She welcomed it more than the hymns that would echo through this space at vespers. In the silence and darkness, there was no reason to hide.

At the end of the corridor, she turned left, then right, before going down a small flight of creaking stairs. The light didn't follow her, but she didn't need it. Her robes vanished in the blackness and only a halo of white from her wimple caught what little light struggled down the stairwell from the hall above. Even the halo faded with each step down.

Her hand reached out into the inky space between her and the old wooden door of cypress honed smooth and damp with age. A striking contrast to the new convent just over her head. Her other hand felt for the cord at her waist and pushed the rosary aside. Deft fingers ran along a second smaller cord looped through the larger one until they grasped a long iron key. She turned it over in her hand, feeling the weight. The age. The roughness. It was strange how so small an object could represent the very place it revealed.

Fingers brushed the face of the door until the cold metal of the lock was felt. Iron on iron grated softly as the key slid into place and turned. As the lock released, the door sighed and crackled open, settling on its rusting hinges. Dampness hissed through the opening and swirled around her with the sweetness of wet earth and herbs. The lamp she had left burning inside the room almost imperceptibly leaped with the rush of air.

A slight turn of the pin at the base of the glass globe pushed the flame higher and bathed the room in warm golden light. Lichen and soft green moss clung to the thick stone walls and floor that had spent decades holding back the depths of the Mississippi surging only a hundred yards away. It shouldn't hold against the push of water from below and the river side, but, mercifully, for some reason it had.

Everything glistened with dampness giving lie to the security of the stone against the water. The lamp sat on the corner of a slick wooden table. Beside it rested a small bell with a frayed bit of string still tied to it and a silver knife with an intricately carved handle. The blade gleamed in the lamplight, except for a ribbon of dark reddish-brown on the tip. She had missed that spot in her rush to clean it but decided to leave it as a reminder of what that blade had done.

A flutter of an eyelid drew her attention to the darkened corner of the room and the shadowy figure that lay there. It was deathly still, except for the eyes that raged beneath closed lids. Searching without seeing.

Mother Micheaux turned her back on the knife and approached the figure lying in the shadows. Breath so slow and shallow, the figure's chest didn't seem to move beneath the dark shroud. Only the head was left uncovered. White skin of the fragile face was lined in a blue web of veins. The only color. Thin gray lips where full red ones should be. Dark lashes twitched against the hollow porcelain cheeks.

Mother Micheaux crooked her finger and pulled a strand of black silken hair away from the pale face. Tears clouded her vision and she could almost see the face for what it should be.

More fluttering of the dark lashes brought the mother superior back to the reason she had come down in the first place. Words. The only words she needed anymore.

She placed one hand across the white forehead and another hand over the heart. At her touch, the eyelids panicked. Flying open, flashing only whites where dark color should have been. Softly, muffled by moss, lichen, and damp, words poured from her mouth onto the soul of the body in the shroud. Words that came without force, without thinking. Words that tasted like blood and fire.

Eyelids calmed and stilled. A flame barely burned. Metal ground against metal. Footsteps faded.

CHAPTER

FOUR

More words surrounded Zéolie, but this time she could catch them in the darkness of her mind. It didn't do any good. She didn't know what they were. They held power but no meaning. They came from nearby in a voice she knew but couldn't remember.

She wanted to see the voice. Her mind raged against her body, willing her eyes to open, but nothing happened. It was dark all the time. She told her hands to push her eyelids open so she could see where she was, but they refused to cooperate.

Most of the time, there was silence, broken only by an occasional soft sputtering sound. Sometimes there were other sounds. Metallic grinding, wood creaking, soft sobbing. Then the words. Soft sobbing, wood creaking, metallic grinding. Silence.

Before the sounds, there was pain. Searing pain in her chest. Burning and heavy. With the words came a shock followed by gentle warmth and an easing of the pain. As it eased, she sank into peace. No words. No pain. Silence and blackness.

When the pain returned before the sounds, she could see strange things behind her eyelids. Fire. A face angry but laughing. Another face pleading, hurt, and crying. Other times there was a storm and a snake. Once, for a moment, there was a woman who moved like water. She smiled and her mossy green eyes danced. A nod, then she was gone.

There were smells, too. Like a swamp, only sweeter. Wet dirt and plants. Lamp oil. And tastes. Water and wine. Blood and fire, like ash and fresh wood. Mostly, there was silence and pain.

"Zéolie?" the words said. "Can you hear me?" The mist had said that before, but this wasn't the mist. She knew the voice. *Yes, yes, I can hear you!* she tried to say. Lips refused to take the shape of the words. "Zéolie, please. Please, *chérie*, come back," the words pleaded.

Zéolie didn't understand, but she couldn't ask the voice what it meant. Her eyes were the only thing that moved. They were the only way she could tell the voice she was already here. If only her damned eyelids would open. She focused her mind on the seemingly simple task that loomed just out of reach. Her mind pulled at them, tugging herself to the surface of the darkness that surrounded her. Reaching for the hidden light on the other side. With a flutter and a jerk, her eyes flew open and were instantly blinded by the lamplight, closing tight once again. *Damnit!* She tried again, this time not so hard. Gently, her eyelids parted, and her eyes rolled forward.

The voice gasped. "Zéolie!"

Slowly, the face above her came into focus. Mother Micheaux.

Tears trickled from the wrinkled edges of the mother superior's eyes as she looked down on the pale girl.

"Can you understand me?" Mother Micheaux asked.

Zéolie blinked wildly.

The aging nun swayed as if she would faint but recovered herself. "What have I done?"

Zéolie wanted answers. Of course, that would mean being able to ask questions. What did the nun mean? What had she done? The words she needed wouldn't come.

Zéolie's dark eyes searched the mother superior's face as the strange dream world began to collide with reality. Camille had touched her. Sent her back. What was it she said? "You aren't finished." Finished with what? It was too much and the darkness began to settle over Zéolie again, pushing her thoughts back into oblivion.

"Drink this," Mother Micheaux said, handing Zéolie a metal cup. Inside was a foul-smelling tea that she never looked forward to. She pushed herself up to sit on the cot and took it. "It's easier if you try to get it in one swallow," the nun said. "I don't know why you try to nurse it like an aged Scotch."

Zéolie rolled her eyes and drank deep, trying not to choke on the liquid that tasted like swamp water and alcohol. For all she knew, that's what it was. The mother superior had been nothing if not vague since Zéolie regained consciousness. There was so little she remembered, and her questions were always met the same way— with blatant evasion.

The nun had at least given her a semblance of an answer when Zéolie asked where she was. "Under the convent. The sisters don't know about this room, so it seemed like a safe place until you're well. There'd be too many questions in the city."

Questions. She had her own questions. The city be damned.

Meals were little better than the drink. Broth. Strange pastes on bread that were oddly similar to the swamp water tea. It didn't matter. She had no appetite. She only ate because Mother Micheaux insisted. The strange concoctions had some purpose other than sustenance, Zéolie was sure of it. She just didn't know what.

One thing that wasn't repulsive was the compress for the scar on her chest. It was healing but hurt like hell any time she moved. She couldn't take a deep breath without sending a shockwave through her. The line stayed red and angry but had finally knit closed enough to stop seeping clear, sticky ooze.

"How long?" Zéolie asked. Her mind was exhausted and her body ached making it hard to put her thoughts into words. Only fragments made it through the pain and confusion.

"How long have you been here?" Mother Micheaux asked. Zéolie shook her head. "How much longer will you be here?" Zéolie nodded. The aging nun stopped crushing herbs in the mortar and pestle and rested her hands on the slick tabletop. She seemed to be searching for words. Zéolie knew what that meant. She wasn't going to get a straight answer this time, either. "There are too many factors for me to say exactly."

The girl squinted at the nun. "How long?" she insisted.

"Soon."

Zéolie shoved the cup at the mother superior and slumped back down on the cot. She didn't have the strength to argue.

"*Chérie*," Mother Micheaux said, "I know you don't want to stay here, but it isn't safe for you. And you've been through so much already."

Zéolie cut her eyes up at the old woman. What had she been through? She didn't even know most of it. Only the little pieces that came to her in the dark.

"Soon," she said again. The mother superior stood and straightened her skirts. "It's almost vespers. I should go before they miss me." She pulled the iron key out of the folds in her habit and Zéolie winced at the sight of it. "I know you don't like it, but I can't risk anyone finding you here. Not yet. You aren't safe yet."

She moved toward the door as Zéolie turned away to the stone wall. Wood creaking, metal grating, footsteps fading. Silence.

CHAPTER

FIVE

Black hair swirled around the woman on the roof of the shack. Behind her, fire raged, eating the trees alive. Yet there was no sound. Only silence. Red lips parted as the woman let loose a silent scream, thrusting her hands forward. Zéolie flew back and slammed to the ground. Without thinking, she balled up her fist and collected tingling energy from the space around her then threw it at the shrieking face. As the ball of light made contact, sound exploded around her. Flames popped and crackled, shrieks echoed in the night, thunder crashed overhead. The cacophony of chaos shook her to her core. Fear washed over her, tempered with strength. She had gathered the power in her hands and threw it. How?

Before she had a chance to figure it out, the madwoman on the roof was hurling more at her. She had to fight or die. That much she knew. Holding her hands out in front of her, she pulled the electricity from the air to send it hurtling at the woman. The woman. Who was she?

As soon as the thought formed, it was answered. It came from a young man lying at her feet. Sandy curls smeared across his sweat-covered brow, fear seizing his dark blue eyes. *There's nothing left of your mother in that madwoman, Zéolie. Kill her.* He hadn't said it. He was too afraid to. Too afraid the woman would hear him. Afraid *her mother* would hear him. *Send her to Hell, if they'll have her*, he thought. *Kill her and you're free.*

Zéolie sent the energy shooting towards the roof knocking the madwoman off her feet. While the maniac struggled, Zéolie dropped to her knees and grabbed the hands of the young man. "Louis?" she asked as the name came to her. He nodded, then began to fade. "No!" she screamed. "Don't go! I—I—" but he was gone. *I love you*, she sobbed into her empty hands.

Something caught the light, glinting at her waist. A knife was tucked into her waistband. Silver with an intricately carved handle. Zéolie pulled it out and turned it over in her hand as the maniac danced and sang on the rooftop. She knew that knife. Her chest began to ache. She knew that knife too well. But why did Mother Micheaux have it?

Dreams held more answers than then cryptic nun, but they were painful and exhausting. Bits and pieces of her past woven with her present. Zéolie was getting stronger every day, and so were the dreams. There were things she knew for sure now and things she still didn't understand. Memories of her mother and the war waged mentally and magically against her flooded back. Solène. Madness and witchcraft in a deadly cocktail. Then there was Louis. Her mother's torture was nothing compared to what Zéolie made him do. And for what? Did it work, or did Solène kill him like she murdered the others?

Zéolie spread her white hands out on the table in front of her. Blue veins wandered over the backs of her hands like tiny rivers on a map. Thin fingers tingled as she stretched them and pulled them back under her palms. Dark eyes drifted over to the silver blade on the other side of the table. She could reach it if she wanted to, but she didn't. Too many times she had seen Mother Micheaux's hand draw back from it. Zéolie knew damn well what she'd tried to do, what Louis had done, with that blade. Why the nun had it when she was so unnerved by it was something Zéolie was determined to find out.

She closed her eyes and pictured the knife across the table. The fingers on her right hand uncurled and hovered just over the surface. She imagined the knife slowly sliding across the expanse of damp wood. A low scraping sound almost broke her concentration, but she clamped her eyes shut and focused on the blade in her mind. Moving so slowly. Cold metal met her palm. Pale fingers closed on the knife as an iron key turned in the lock.

Zéolie's eyes opened to the look of panic on the mother superior's face in the dark doorway.

"What are you doing?" the nun hissed as she thrust the door closed behind her.

Zéolie tightened her grip on the handle of the knife. "I think it's time you answered that question."

For a long moment, the two women stared across the dancing lamplight in silence, both waging their own internal battles. Youth conquered age, and the old nun sighed as she lowered her eyes. "Fine. Just let go of the knife first."

Zéolie opened her hand and the knife slid back across the table where it had been. A small gasp escaped the lips of the nun and her eyes searched Zéolie for an explanation. None came. The young woman silently waited for the nun to confess.

Mother Micheaux sat down and settled her skirt, her hand absently fidgeting with her rosary. "What do you want to know?"

Zéolie leveled her gaze at the old woman. "Who are you?" It wasn't one of the questions she had wanted to ask for so long. Those seemed distant now. Sitting across from the woman she thought she knew, the question materialized and left her mouth on its own. None of the other questions mattered if she didn't know who she was talking to.

"You know who I am," the nun dodged.

"Do I?" Zéolie parried.

Mother Micheaux sighed. "No." Silence hung like lead between them as the aging nun figured out where to start her confession. "What you know about me is true, but that isn't all," she began. "Once I entered the convent walls, I became Sister Marie Ste. Joseph Micheaux. A young nun eager to serve the Lord. That was what the other sisters were told. A young French noble come to serve the Church. I was sixteen when I was sent here to join the Order. I was sixteen when I..." her voice faltered, then she finished, "killed a boy."

Zéolie's eyes narrowed, but she said nothing. Her heart beat harder in her aching chest as the nun's last three words rang in her ears.

"There was a reason I was so close to your mother, why the Mother Superior was, too, when she and Camille arrived. She wasn't the first of her kind to seek refuge in the convent." Her breathing became shallow and quick as she spoke. Years of silence about who and what she was crumbled around her. "Like your family, generations of my ancestors have been touched by powers and abilities that were once prized but came to be feared. There was no rhyme or reason to it. From what we know of your family, it seems to be a direct line of women. Our family couldn't predict who would be born with it. My father had the gift, if you could call it that, and passed it to me.

"As early as I can remember, he would read with me, teaching me the old words. No one knew where they'd come from. He had books with drawings and incantations that had been passed down, but always told me that the words others used weren't as powerful as the ones we chose for ourselves."

"I've heard them," Zéolie said softly.

Mother Micheaux nodded. "Yes. Those words are more powerful than anything I'd ever known. My father would take me away from the house and prying eyes of the servants to work on using the words."

"Here?"

"Here. He'd built this place when he came to New Orleans. Years later, the rest of the building was constructed above. It seemed odd to me that he never used the gift he possessed but treated it more like an heirloom to be taken out once in a while, looked at with reverence, then hidden away for safekeeping. On the day I entered the convent, I knew why."

"The boy?" Zéolie asked, her voice a broken whisper.

Mother Micheaux seemed to drift away as she talked of that day. "My father gave me a beautiful mare that I loved to ride along the river. I was the only one who could handle her. She'd shy away from or nip at anyone else who would try to touch her. While I was in the courtyard tending to the herb garden, one of the slave boys was cleaning the stable of our carriage horse and got too close to my mare in the next stall. She nipped his ear and he turned the whip on her, lashing her across the face. The mare reared in pain, knocking him back as blood ran down between her beautiful eyes. Rage flooded me as she whinnied and kicked at him in fear. Before I knew what I'd done, the boy was dead. A gaping hole in his chest. Hurting my precious horse had ripped my heart out, and with a word and an outstretched hand, I'd done the same to him from across the courtyard." Sobs racked her frail body as she struggled to catch her breath. Zéolie said nothing, letting the woman have time with her grief.

After a few minutes, Mother Micheaux recovered enough to go on. "Father blamed the horse, making it seem as though the horse had kicked the boy in the chest. It was a believable enough lie since there was blood all over the stable, including her hooves. The horse was shot for good measure and I was sent to the one place Father hoped would keep the gift in check. And, as a nun, the family inheritance would end with me."

"Seems a drastic thing to do over the death of a slave," Zéolie said. Laws in New Orleans were strict concerning the treatment of slaves, but that certainly didn't eliminate all abuse. An accident with a horse wouldn't have raised any charges. "Why was he so willing to trade the life of that boy for his daughter's future?"

"Fear. If I was capable of losing control like that, he was afraid of what else might happen. And who might find out. My future wasn't as important as securing the noble legacy for the rest of my siblings. He couldn't risk being found out for what he was because of a mistake I might make."

"New Orleans has her share of eccentrics. Surely, here, of all places, would be the one place he might have some security if the secret came out?"

The nun shook her head. "His title came from the French crown. The king wouldn't be as forgiving as the city of New Orleans might've been." Mother Micheaux continued, "Coming into the convent, I vowed I'd never use the gift that flowed through my veins. Guilt over what I'd done consumed me, and I promised God I'd purge those words with the words of prayers. For years, it worked, but the old words would never leave me completely. They swirled through my dreams, wove their way into songs I would sing to myself as I did chores. Always there.

"When the diocese decided to relocate the Ursulines, Fate brought us here, to the building on top of Father's chamber. It was as though my gift wasn't finished with me yet." She paused and looked at Zéolie. "And it wasn't."

Zéolie's gaze settled on the worn face of the nun, weighing whether or not this was the entirety of the story. Something told her there was more, but the last words rang in her head. "Not finished. Camille said the same thing before you brought me back." Zéolie's hands went to her temples as she asked the question she wasn't sure she wanted an answer to. "Louis? What happened to Louis?"

The nun shook her head. "I don't know."

"My mother? Is she gone?"

A deep sigh came from the depths of the nun. "She's gone, yes, but I couldn't tell you if it was for good."

"Then what did Camille mean?"

"That, *chérie*, is between you and your grandmother. I have no idea."

For the first time, Zéolie was certain the nun had told her the whole truth.

CHAPTER

SIX

Lisette squealed with joy and valiantly resisted the urge to rush at Zéolie the instant she saw her. Celeste grinned, but made no move toward her, either. Madame Marchon stood regally between them in the empty foyer of the Cheval house on Dauphine Street. "Welcome home, *chérie*," she said with a warm smile. Her voice echoed in the hollowness of the room and for a moment, Zéolie longed for the small coziness of the damp convent chamber.

The mother superior had put Madame Marchon in charge of renovations to the Cheval house during Zéolie's convalescence. Certain rooms in particular. Rooms, like her father's, that still held echoes of a painful past. Julien Cheval's bedroom furniture had been removed, taken to the swamp, and burned. The foyer furniture was gone, too, and the walls repainted to a cheerful yellow. It was as close to daylight as Zéolie had seen yet. The darkness of night was more comforting to her after so long in the small room under the convent. It would take time for her to adjust to the brightness of day.

. . .

19

THE WOMEN, who had known Zéolie almost her entire life, had been warned of the change in her, but it did little to prepare them for the pale beauty with the sunken eyes that stood before them. Despite Mother Micheaux's efforts, color was stubborn about returning to Zéolie's skin. Her paleness marked her as a soul who cheated death. Even with a thick coating of powder, shadows of veins still ran across her face. Her lips were tinted to cover the gray, but it was garish compared to the soft deep pink that had been there before.

Zéolie knew what she looked like. A face she had seen dancing on a rooftop in the swamp. Color still eluded her complexion, but her strength had returned.

No one seemed to know what to do with themselves, or what to say in those first moments. The last time the three of them had seen Zéolie was at her funeral. She didn't look much different now, except that she was standing up.

"You look like you've seen a ghost," Zéolie said, trying to lighten the awkwardness.

"We did! You *died*!" Lisette blurted, then blushed crimson to the roots of her hair.

Madame Marchon put a hand on her daughter's arm. "That's quite enough." She took a step towards Zéolie and smiled. "You're just in time to help me make some decisions."

"But first, there's something you'll want to see." Madame Marchon led Zéolie to the back of the house and out the door to the courtyard.

There, in the moonlight, was the wheel of plants she set out with her aunt, Mama Nell. They had grown into a full healthy garden, green and lush. Zéolie turned tear-filled eyes to Madame Marchon and the smiling girls behind her. "It's beautiful," she whispered.

Celeste grinned at her friend. "I've developed quite a talent for gardening, don't you think?"

Lisette elbowed her sister out of the way. "You? I did most of it. You just stood around and pointed."

"I make a fabulous supervisor," Celeste said smugly.

"Girls," Madame Marchon said, gently and effectively ending the bickering.

Zéolie beamed at the women. "Thank you. You have no idea what this means to me."

They really didn't. To them, it was her connection to the aunt she loved. To Zéolie it was so much more. It was lessons, power, and protection. Things she was going to need desperately if Camille was right.

"We'll keep tending it for you," Lisette said, "until you're all better and back at home for good."

"Which will be longer than it should be unless we get some things taken care of," Madame Marchon said. She led them back into the house, then to the parlor. "Now then." Madame Marchon settled into the creaking chair behind the desk. Next to the lamp was a piece of paper with the list of party preparations she had made with the help of the Marchon girls.

Zéolie's mind drifted back to the night she and the girls worked on the list for her birthday party after her other lists went missing. The tarot cards. The Hanged Man. Warnings she should have seen.

The next hour passed with Madame Marchon going through the changes to the house. She asked Zéolie's opinion, and Zéolie asked hers. Whatever Madame Marchon said was the decision made. Truthfully, Zéolie didn't care about any of it. The house was thick with ghosts of her past, no matter what furniture was in it or what color the walls were. It was a past she'd need to come to grips with, not run from.

THE DAMP STONE room under the convent had become more home to her than the mansion on Dauphine. It was freeing to be away from a world of questions and confusion. Rumors flew about what had happened the night she died and the months following that ranged from the truth to the outlandish. Mother Micheaux had done her best to make sure the most heard rumor was the one she wanted told: Zéolie was injured trying to help Louis, who was in the swamp following a lead for clues to her father's death. She'd lost so much blood that the physicians pronounced her dead. Grieving friends unable to come to grips with that had placed a safety bell, usually only used with yellow fever victims, on her coffin, which saved her life. Because of the fragileness of her condition and the yellow fever in the hospitals, she was being treated by the nuns in the convent infirmary. Just enough truth to make it believable.

As the house was renovated and rumors were spread, Zéolie immersed herself in the words of Mother Micheaux's father. She was damned if the gift was going to end with an old nun. The words had brought Zéolie back, and they would finish whatever it was she came back to do. With the nun's help, words were deciphered, committed to memory, and sparred with. The mother superior was one hell of a dueling partner when it came to slinging spells around a tiny dank room.

By the time the house was finished, color had returned to Zéolie's cheeks with only shadows of the map of veins as a souvenir of her death. And her strength had returned. All of it.

SEVEN

" I just don't like it, Zéolie," Mother Micheaux said to the floor of the convent parlor. She had lost the girl once, and she didn't know how well she could protect her again.

Zéolie smiled warmly at the nun who had given back her life. "I can't keep hiding under the convent. Not if you want your story to be believed. If I never come back, the stories of my death will only get worse." Zéolie sighed. "You'd think people would get tired of all this."

Mother Micheaux shook her head and pulled the curtains aside like she had done several times already. She searched the convent grounds, but for what, she couldn't say. The veil she wore seemed to droop heavy across her shoulders as she gazed outside. Caring for Zéolie would have been enough to wear her out, but the practicing had almost done the old woman in. "Something will distract the city soon enough, but until it does, you'll be the talk of every tongue-wagger in the Quarter." She paused. "It's not rumors and gossip that I'm afraid of."

"I know that." Zéolie took the frail hands of the mother superior in her own. While the nun seemed slightly hunched and small, the young woman in front of her was statuesque, even wearing the borrowed clothes of one of the novices for the second time. "You've done all you can, and I know it's more than enough. I can *do this*." She squeezed the wrinkled hands that trembled slightly against her palms.

Mother Micheaux nodded. "I know. I just—" There was no sense in arguing or trying to protect a young woman whose strength surpassed her own. She couldn't hold Zéolie back because of her own guilt. "I know," she said again returning the squeeze before drawing her hands away.

"Mother Micheaux?" a timid voice said from the parlor doorway.

"Yes, sister?" the mother superior asked.

"The carriage is ready."

"Thank you." The novice nodded and went quickly down the hall. "The Marchons will stay with you for a while. Several of their servants, too," Mother Micheaux said with the voice of someone accustomed to being in charge of others. Despite her exhaustion, she was still in command of the situation. "You know how to brew the tea. I'll keep blending the herbs for you." Zéolie wrinkled her nose at the mention of the swamp water tea. "It doesn't matter how much you hate it, you'll need it for a while longer."

"How much longer?" Zéolie asked.

Mother Micheaux traced a blue vein on her cheek. "A while."

"Fine," Zéolie said.

The nun nodded. "I'll be over soon to get what I need from the garden. Nell must've known you'd need it."

Zéolie's heart ached at the mention of Mama Nell. Her caramel skin and dancing mossy eyes haunted Zéolie's dreams. It was a stark contrast to the image of the priestess' contorted face and foaming mouth that was seared into Zéolie's memory. "She must have. I wish I knew what to do with everything she planted."

"You will. Her books are still there." Mother Micheaux put a hand on Zéolie's arm. "As hard as it is for me to say, it's time." She said it but made no move toward the door.

"After you," Zéolie said with a forced smile of reassurance.

As much as the mother superior and Madame Marchon tried to orchestrate a clandestine return to Dauphine Street for Zéolie, her arrival spread like rumors will do in the closeness of the Quarter. Hard on the heels of the news were invitations to luncheons, dinner parties, and all manner of ways to get the resurrected beauty into the finest parlors in New Orleans. Madame Marchon put Lisette to work writing polite refusals to each of them while Celeste was entertained by mocking the pretentious cards that accompanied the ridiculous amounts of flowers being delivered every day.

"It's like a florist in here," Zéolie said cracking open a window to let some of the thick perfume out.

Celeste snorted. "You didn't have this many flowers at your funeral."

Lisette's hand stopped and hovered just above the note she was writing. "That's such a strange thing to say to someone, don't you think? I mean, how often do you get to talk to someone about what was at their funeral?"

"I admit, it's a rare discussion," Celeste said, rolling her eyes at her sister. The front doorbell jangled, and Celeste plopped a long lily stem into the center of an arrangement. "I'll get it. I'm sure it's another addition to the indoor garden party." Her hips swayed as she sauntered to the door in no hurry to deal with one more flower delivery.

When Celeste didn't come right back with a spray of flowers, Zéolie peeked around the salon door frame into the foyer. The long lazy figure of Celeste was leaning with her shoulder against the door, one hip slung out to the side and her hand at her waist. Her other hand was twirling a curl around her finger. Celeste would flirt with almost anything with a pulse, but she reserved this pose for only a select few. Surely, she wasn't throwing it away on a florist's delivery boy.

"No, I wish I could help you, and I do mean that," Celeste said silkily, "but there isn't anyone at this address by that name."

The silhouette on the other side of the doorway shifted awkwardly. Tall, thin, and obviously unsure what to do with the blatant flirtation in front of him. As much fun as it would have been to see where Celeste took it, Zéolie stepped in before Madame Marchon got an eyeful of her daughter making a pass at the young stranger.

"Maybe I can help?" she asked.

Celeste sashayed back into the parlor, stopping to grumble, "You're no fun," in Zéolie's ear as she passed.

Zéolie smiled at the visitor which disarmed him even more than Celeste had.

"I—I don't know. I was given this address, but there seems to be a mistake," said the young man in an odd mix of New Orleans drawl and refined French accents. His eyes traveled over Zéolie. Nervously, he swallowed hard and searched for anything else to look at other than the woman in the doorway.

"Come on into the parlor. Maybe between all of us, we can figure out how to help you," Zéolie said, trying her best to put the flustered young man at ease. He was dressed formally, more in the European style than the casualness of New Orleans. The fabrics of his trousers and waistcoat were far too warm for the subtropical climate of the city. "How long have you been in New Orleans?" she asked in an attempt at small talk.

"What?" he asked, startled. "How—how did you know?"

"Your clothes. They seem a bit...warm for New Orleans this time of year."

"Or any time of year, really," Celeste chimed in. "I still say everyone should just go around naked in the summer. Well, maybe not *every*one." Her mother shot her a warning look that quelled any more comments for the time being.

Madame Marchon came around the desk where she was overseeing Lisette's letters and held a hand out to the young man. "Shall we start again on the right foot?" she asked with a warm smile that seemed to settle him. The fine manners of an older woman sat better with him than flirtations of beautiful girls. "Madame Marchon. And these are my girls, Lisette and Celeste," she said as each one gave a polite nod. "And this is Zéolie Cheval, the mistress of the house."

Zéolie dropped a slight curtsey and held her hand out to the young man. He took it with a small bow and said, "Julien Haydel." The look on Zéolie's face shook the young man's confidence again. "I —I'm sorry. I didn't mean to—"

She recovered herself and smiled. "No, no. It's nothing you did. My father's name was Julien. He recently"—she faltered—"recently passed away."

Julien Haydel blushed deep red to the roots of his black hair. "I— I'm sorry to hear that." His weight shifted from one foot to the other as he outwardly struggled with how to handle himself.

Madame Marchon swept to his rescue once again. "Come, have a seat and we'll see what we can do to help you. Lisette, would you pour a drink for our guest? Brandy, perhaps?" She directed the last question to Julien, who nodded.

Zéolie offered him a chair and settled herself next to Celeste on the settee, certain she'd need to pinch her at some point to keep the girl in check with their uncomfortable, but boyishly handsome, guest. "Now, from what little I gathered at the door, you're looking for someone?"

Julien took the glass offered to him by Lisette and smiled shyly at her. She blushed and went back to the desk. "My mother," he said after a sip of the brandy. "Marie Haydel. I haven't heard from her in years, and when I finally do, she gives me the wrong address."

"Haydel," Madame Marchon said, leaning back in her chair. She held her fingertips together and tapped them in thought. "There's the Haydel plantation, but that's half a day's ride from here at least."

"Maybe this'll help," he said, pulling a letter out of his vest pocket. "It's not much to go on, but it's all I have from her."

Zéolie took the paper and unfolded it. The page was soft and worn as if the young man had read and folded it a hundred times. "You're right. This is the address on the letter."

"That's odd," Madame Marchon said. "Maybe the numbers are reversed?"

"Possibly," Zéolie said quietly. "Maybe she's staying with someone? A friend?"

Julien's thoughts clouded his brow. "Maybe." He sighed and leaned back in the chair, resting his glass on his knee.

Celeste leaned forward and grinned, a curl wound tight around her long finger. "I'd be happy to go knocking on doors with you until you find her." Her words were satin in her mouth and Julien squirmed in his chair. He glanced at Madame Marchon who clicked her tongue in disapproval of her daughter's wantonness. "Then again," Celeste said flopping back against the settee in a huff, "I'll probably have flowers to tend to."

Julien looked around the parlor noticing the abundance of arrangements for the first time. "You certainly do seem to have your hands full."

Lisette found the courage to speak. "That's because everyone's so glad Zéolie's a"—her mother poked her in the ribs—"feeling better," she corrected. Abashed, Lisette sank back into silence.

"You know," Celeste said steering the conversation back to the matter at hand, "it'd help if we knew a little more about your mother."

Julien stared at his feet. "It would. And I'd love to tell you more, but there isn't much I can say."

Madame Marchon stepped in. "Monsieur Haydel, please excuse Celeste. Manners have never been her strength." Celeste blushed, but rolled her eyes at her mother. "We'd never think of prying into your family affairs. I'm sure there's another way to help you."

"It isn't because it's private," he said. "Nothing like that. I just don't know much about her. And nothing at all of my father."

"That does make this a bit more difficult," Zéolie conceded. "You said you haven't heard from her in years?"

Julien shook his head. "No, I haven't. When I was little, I went to live with relatives in France. My aunt always said my mother wanted me to have a good education so she sent me to them but wouldn't ever say anything else about her. Once in a while, I'd get a letter from my mother, but they always seemed like a formality. 'Hope you're well. Work hard in school. I'll see you soon.' Same thing almost every time. Nothing at all that would help now."

Madame Marchon leaned forward in her chair. "Do you have them? Was there an address that might help?"

Julien shook his head. A strand of black hair fell across his forehead and he pushed it back in place. "No. I wish I did. Since I had this address, I left the rest in France."

"Great," Celeste groaned. "That's helpful. My knocking on doors idea is looking better and better."

Zéolie laughed. "You may be right."

Julien drained the brandy in his glass. The alcohol steadied his nerves, and he was settling out of his embarrassed awkwardness. "I might have to resort to that. At least I'd have good company."

The corner of Celeste's mouth turned up in a half-grin and Zéolie was quite certain the thoughts in her head weren't exactly wholesome. "The best," Celeste said with a flicker of a wink at the young man. For a moment, he let his eyes settle on her face and the edges of his lips curled into a smile before remembering his manners and the presence of Celeste's mother.

"We'd all help, if it came to that," Zéolie said, cooling the fire in her friend. "But I'm sure it won't."

"Pity," Celeste smirked crossing one long leg over the other.

Julien grinned again, but didn't encourage her. Instead, he turned his attention to Zéolie. "I appreciate you trying to help, but I've intruded on your hospitality long enough." He stood to go and held a hand out to her. "I'm sorry my mother isn't here. It would've given me a good reason to stay."

Zéolie gave him her hand and he bent over it, brushing his lips gently over the back of her hand. As he stood, Zéolie met his dark eyes with a dazzling smile that almost shook his new-found finesse. "You're welcome anytime," she said gracefully. "It's been a pleasure."

"Oh, I assure you, Mademoiselle Cheval, the pleasure's been mine." With a bow to the other ladies, he followed Zéolie to the front door.

"I hope you find your mother. She must be worried about you." Zéolie opened the door and leaned on the doorframe as Julien fidgeted with his watch chain. "If there's anything I can do..." she trailed off thinking of ways she could help the young man if only she didn't have to worry about being found out for what she really was.

"Your kindness has been plenty," Julien said smiling warmly down at her. "After all these years, coming back here not knowing anyone..."

Zéolie laughed. "You changed that with one ring of a doorbell. You're going to be just fine here."

Julien grinned and took his leave of her. She slowly closed the door watching him disappear into the deep evening shadows between the French Quarter mansions.

By the time Zéolie made it back to the parlor, Lisette was giggling, and Celeste was fanning herself pretending to faint over the arm of the settee while their mother tsked and rolled her eyes at their silliness.

"Of all the houses he could've come to!" Celeste said fanning down the front of her bodice.

"That's enough," Madame Marchon said firmly. "Up to bed with you."

"Who can sleep?" Lisette asked grinning.

Zéolie said nothing as the girls giggled their way upstairs. She knew how they felt. She felt the same way when the fog around her father's death began to clear and she found Louis at her side. Zéolie shut her eyes tight against the images of him that flashed in her memories hovering around the edges of sleep. Instead, she forced her favorite vision of him to mind. Dark sandy curls falling onto his forehead as he caught her in the hallway of the convent when she tripped over her skirt. How she wanted to fall into his arms again. But it was her fault that she couldn't. She made him kill her. She died and left him to that maniac. *Louis, what the hell happened? What did she do to you?*

Zéolie pushed her bedroom door open and fell across her new bed crying tears she couldn't stop with all the magic in her veins.

CHAPTER

EIGHT

"At least the florist has done well in all this," Mother Micheaux said, surveying the abundance of flowers in the parlor.

"And these are just the ones we didn't put in the bedrooms and dining room." Zéolie sighed. "They've taken over the house."

The mother superior laughed. "Now they can take over the pauper's cemetery instead. I'm sure the dead will appreciate them. Sister Mary Margaret?" she called to a nun waiting for instructions in the foyer.

With a furtive glance at Zéolie as she came in, the nun asked, "Yes, Mother?"

"You and Sister Rosalie can bring all of these to the carriage. Once it's loaded, go on to the cemetery. I'll be here a while longer."

The nun nodded and glanced nervously once more at Zéolie on her way out.

"When are they going to stop looking at me like that?" Zéolie asked, rolling her eyes.

Mother Micheaux shook her head. "Can you blame them, really?" she asked, absently running a finger along a lily stem. "The sisters

32

were the ones who prepared your body. I couldn't let them do anything but clean up the blood, dress the wound, and put clean clothes on you. Nothing about your burial was normal, so they're suspicious. I trust them to keep their thoughts to themselves, but I can't control their expressions. You were dead, and they know it."

Sister Rosalie came into the parlor with a large wicker basket to gather the smaller arrangements, putting an end to the conversation. She went silently to work while Zéolie and Mother Micheaux pulled drooping blooms out of sprays around the room. Once the flowers were loaded and the carriage on its way through the Quarter, Zéolie and Mother Micheaux got down to the real work of finding out what Camille meant about not being finished yet.

The small round table Mama Nell first used to teach Zéolie candle magic was brought to the center of the room and draped in a white cloth. "The basket's with the still," Mother Micheaux said as she smoothed a crease out of the fabric.

"I'll get it," Zéolie volunteered. She had avoided the kitchen with Mama Nell's oil still since she moved back into the house. Madame Marchon's servants were instructed not to use Zéolie's kitchen and spent the past week bringing food through the Quarter from their house. It seemed cumbersome to them, but they never balked at their mistress' orders.

Zéolie walked through the courtyard that was rapidly being consumed by her garden. Most of the plants were growing almost out of control except for the ones that were ingredients in the vile concoction of swamp tea that was bringing her color and strength back. She ran her fingers through the rosemary and lavender, letting the rich aromas hover around her on the heavy air. In the back of her mind, her aunt's words softly told her what each plant was magically and medically capable of. Fragrant green power and protection. It was all just a jumble of words now.

Past the garden, at the rear of the courtyard, was the kitchen. Wavy glass panes collected dew from the humid morning air. Drops raced each other to the wooden frame leaving muddy trails in their wakes. Through the glass, she could make out the clunky shape of the small oil still draped in cloth. Zéolie stood on the threshold for a moment with her hand on the warm wooden door. She'd hoped somehow Mama Nell would be the one picking up the lessons where she left off, but she was gone and Zéolie was the reason why.

Pushing down the lump that was forming in her throat, Zéolie eased the door open. Dust twinkled in the sunlight like fairy dust as fresh air filtered in. In the mustiness, she could smell kerosene and an earthiness of the herbs that had been prepared there.

She found the wicker basket in the corner of the room, tucked next to the still. The metal contraption of hodgepodge pieces seemed to whisper to her about oils and herbs, but she couldn't understand any of it. This was Mama Nell's world, not hers.

Sighing under the weight of all she still had to learn, Zéolie hooked her arm through the handle of the basket. Even this seemed heavier than it should be. She had power inside of her, but there was so much she needed to know. So much that could protect her from needing the power she possessed.

Carrying Nell's things back to the house, guilt and pain settled deeper and deeper into her mind. How could she work with the candles and tools that Mama Nell kept in this basket, the one brought to the house by Vernand who loved Nell more than his whole world, when even being near them submerged her mind into the depths of her grief? Leaden steps carried her back into the parlor and her next lesson.

Mother Micheaux stood in silence as Zéolie set the basket on the table. It was as though she anticipated the effect the walk to the kitchen would have on the young woman. With reverence usually reserved for holy communion, the mother superior lifted the large white candle out of the basket. Sigils carved into it so many months and a lifetime ago sent chills through Zéolie. The last time she saw those witch's symbols, they had been carved into the flesh of the man she loved.

"I can't do this," Zéolie whispered staring at the carved wax.

"You don't have a choice," Mother Micheaux answered flatly. "Neither of us do anymore. If Camille says you still have work to do, we need to know exactly what she meant." She set the candle on the brass stand from the basket and began to place stones and shells around the center candle. "Shells for protection, crystals for clarity, and sage for cleansing. She thought of everything." A slow deep breath rattled through aging lungs. It seemed to fight against her as she pulled it in. Nell thought of everything, but one thing wasn't in the basket. It was tucked into the nun's robe.

Age-spotted hands trembled slightly as she flexed her fingers, not wanting to touch the blade that took the life of the young woman across from her. Another strained breath chased the first one out of her chest as her fingertips brushed the cold handle. Struggling with her own demons, she gripped the knife and pulled it out of the black folds. The lined face of the nun was contorted with emotion as she laid it next to the center candle.

Zéolie knew the pain the blade held for the mother superior as the symbol of what forced her back into a life she had sought to leave behind, but there was no way in hell the nun could feel the torment Zéolie felt. Pain mingled with power as her hand hovered over the carved handle. Beauty, strength, magic, evil. All in one slender silver knife. The blade that carved the sigils in the candle, the blade that carved Louis' skin, the blade that killed her.

As Zéolie's fingers rested on the cool metal, images thundered into her mind. She wanted to collapse into them but knew she could easily lose herself in their vortex. Camille had said Zéolie wasn't finished, and who knew how much time she had to prepare for whatever was coming at her? Wallowing in misery wasn't a luxury she could afford.

"Ready or not," Zéolie whispered.

Mother Micheaux nodded. "Sit there," she said tapping the opposite side of the table and took the chair across from Zéolie.

"We've tried this before at the convent and it's never worked. There's just too much...in the way." Zéolie's internal struggle was written all over her face. Dark eyes darting but unfocused, mouth drawn tight, and creases forming between her black eyebrows.

Mother Micheaux could live with those things, but there was one manifestation of the strain that she wasn't comfortable with. Zéolie's face had gone white and blue veins streaked across her cheeks. "Do you have the strength for this?"

"What choice do I have?"

"If the practice wears you out too much, how will you have enough strength if you need to fight?"

Zéolie sighed, drawing in as much energy from around her as she could and releasing the pain that was blocking her focus. If she didn't have the strength within her, she'd have to pull it from around her. Even that had its drawback. She could only hold onto that energy for so long before it began to fight against her to be released. Once she let it go, she'd be more exhausted. "I can do it," was her only answer.

Mother Micheaux stared back at her, unsure how much of that was determination and how much was foolishness. Knowing she couldn't stop Zéolie once the girl set her mind on something, the nun got to work. Controlling as much of the tremor that had settled into her hands as she could, she lit the center candle. The flame popped and sputtered as if irritated at being woken from a long sleep before settling into a steady burn. Golden light pooled in the middle of the table in the darkness of the drawn curtains, even though the mid-morning sun was singeing the French Quarter rooftops outside.

Zéolie closed her eyes and flattened her hands on the tablecloth, trying to will the thoughts swirling through her mind back into oblivion. One by one, Nell, Louis, and her mother faded as she concentrated everything on Camille. There wasn't much to concentrate on besides silvery mist and the voice that seemed so far away now. Words began to fill the space around her as Mother Micheaux spoke. From her lips fell words that were becoming more and more part of Zéolie's fabric. Rising and falling. Weaving in and out of her consciousness. Clear and strong. Faint and whispered. Sage smoke filled the room as the herb burned and cleansed the space, grounding the words in earthiness.

Slowly, the blackness in Zéolie's mind gave way to swirling mist. She knew this place. She'd been here before, but it seemed so long ago. For the first time since they began attempting this exercise, the images of her grief dissipated and allowed the mist to come through.

"Camille?" Zéolie whispered. Nothing. Just swirling mist.

The mother superior's words echoed in the empty space.

"Please..." Zéolie begged the mist around her. "Please, Camille. I need you." Mist began to pull together becoming opaque, tightening around her. Shimmering. Pulsing. Silent.

More words, but nothing from the mist.

"I know you're here, Camille," Zéolie told the mist. "I need you to talk to me." Shimmering silence. "Please. Tell me what I haven't finished. What do you need me to do?" She had asked the question to darkness and swirling memories every other time she tried to reach her grandmother. It never worked. She couldn't focus enough to find Camille. With the mist gathered in front of her, she was closer than she'd ever been, but still nothing. No answer. Frustration built in her and the mist began to dissipate. "No!" she shouted into the void. "Don't go!" But the mist was vanishing. As it did, a soft chuckle danced through her mind, low and menacing, then gone.

Zéolie's eyes flew open, pulling herself out of the vision. The echo of the laugh she knew too well rang in her ears. "Nothing!" she snarled as frustration got the better of her. Glass shattered and brass clanked onto the wood floor as Zéolie cleared the mantle of vases and candlesticks with a wave of her hand.

Mother Micheaux looked calmly at her from across the table. "You're going to have to get control of that."

"What?" Zéolie snapped.

"Your temper. You can't throw a magical tantrum every time you get frustrated. Not that I liked those candlesticks," the mother superior answered dryly.

Zéolie rolled her eyes. With a flick of a finger, she put the candlesticks back in their place. Shards of glass danced into the fireplace.

"And keep that sass in check, too." The nun cut her eyes at Zéolie. "The vases weren't half bad."

Zéolie sighed and the glass swirled out of the fire grate and reassembled on the mantle.

"That's better. If you're going to lose control, you better be able to clean up your messes. And remember that there are some things you can't fix again." Mother Micheaux stared hard at Zéolie.

Nell's contorted face flashed in front of Zéolie's. Beautiful features twisted in shock and pain as her body absorbed Zéolie's angry misfire. "I'm sorry," she answered quietly. "It's just—" She couldn't say it. It couldn't have been real.

The nun's face softened. "What, *chérie?*"

Zéolie's dark eyes closed tight as she tried to push the sound of that laugh away. She shook her head. "I—I heard her."

"Camille? But you said—"

Zéolie held up a hand to stop her. "No, not Camille. I heard my mother laughing at me. Low and hollow."

Color drained from Mother Micheaux's face. "No," she whispered. "She's gone. It couldn't have been Solène."

"I can't forget that sound. It was definitely her. But there was something different. Her laugh was more like an echo, floating lifeless across an expanse."

The aging nun tensed. "It couldn't have been her. Your mind wasn't focused." Her words darted around the room. Unsettled. Nervous. Hopeful they were truth, but worried they were lies. After a moment, they found Zéolie and clung to her.

"Maybe you're right. Maybe I wasn't focused." But it didn't make sense. Even at her most scattered, with images of her past flashing like lightning through her mind, Zéolie had never heard that laugh. She'd seen the images of her mother's madness at the edges of sleep, but not when she was trying to channel Camille. Something about this wasn't right. Something had changed.

Mother Micheaux's hand hovered for an instant above the knife on the table before moving over to the crystals and stones. One by one, she lifted each one carefully and placed them in the basket. The candle was snuffed and set upright in the corner of the basket for the wax to cool and solidify. "We'll try again, but not today." She looked at the drawn face of the beautiful young woman across from her. Blue veins streaking across pale skin. "You need your tea. And some rest."

CHAPTER

NINE

Shadows stretched and yawned through the narrow spaces between the buildings of the French Quarter as the sun settled itself on the horizon. Lamps and candles glowed in windows, warding off the coming night. The clattering sounds of day gave way to the silkier sounds of night, broken only by music wafting over the rooftops from bars and brothels. At the end of one of those bars, a young man sat absently dragging a fingertip around the rim of a glass. His other hand ran through dark hair, pushing it back from his face. On the aging wooden bar next to a water ring was a folded piece of paper. The ink was smudged in places where sweating hands had gripped it too tight. Words wept at their own uselessness.

Throwing back the end of his drink, the young man stuffed the paper into his waistcoat and tossed some coins on the bar. Even the wink of the Creole waitress as he passed her did nothing to lift the weight of frustration that chained his spirit down.

Long strides carried him into the darkness that caressed the cooling port city. Fog from the river sashayed down darkened streets, dancing with pools of lamplight only to flit from partner to partner. He walked with purpose toward no destination. Every one of the close French Quarter streets were nothing more to him than dead ends, yet he trudged relentlessly after them.

Day after day, Julien Haydel walked the streets hoping someone knew his mother. Every time he mentioned her name, it was the same response he received from the Marchons. "There's the Haydel plantation half a day's ride from here, but no one by that name in the city." Occasionally, someone would good-naturedly send him on an unintentional wild goose chase. As he walked the darkened streets of the city more than slightly inebriated, two thoughts took turns occupying his mind. The first was the possibility of someone making a fool of him with this quest for a mother who didn't want to be found. The second was the smiling dark eyes of the mistress of the Cheval house.

She haunted his thoughts for reasons he couldn't understand. He was drawn to the gravity of the dark-haired beauty. There was none of the flamboyance of the Parisian women or the crassness of the harbor harlots who had been the two dominant threads of his adolescent fabric. Fantasies of what men thought they wanted. Zéolie was what women should be. Poise, beauty, and strength with smiling eyes.

Yet there was something strange about her. Something he couldn't figure out even as often as she permeated his thoughts. Shadows of veins like delicate streams flowing just beneath the surface of porcelain skin. Guarded eyes that smiled but watched everything. Power unusual for a woman of her young years sizzling under her gentle grace. Magnetic.

Each time her face found its way into Julien's thoughts, he only let it linger for a moment. Each time a moment longer than the last. She was a distraction he didn't have time for. There was an urgency in his mother's words and his first priority was finding her, even if she wasn't helping at all.

"It's like she doesn't want to be found," he grumbled to the rising moon.

"Her loss," a feminine voice said.

Julien spun around, but no one was there. A soft chuckle tumbled gently from above. Stepping off the banquette and into the street, he looked up at the wrought-iron gallery above him. There, leaning on her arms crossed on the railing, was a dark-haired beauty whose pale skin almost shimmered in the moonlight. Zéolie. Without realizing it, he walked his way to the Cheval house on Dauphine.

Once he remembered to close his mouth, he swept his hat from his head and gave her a graceful bow. "Mademoiselle Cheval," he said as he rose.

She smiled down at him. "I'm sorry, I didn't mean to startle you. You seemed pretty deep into your own thoughts coming down the block, but I couldn't resist saying something."

"I'm glad you did," Julien answered, grinning up at her.

"There's one more glass of wine left," she said, holding a green bottle up to the moonlight and examining the deep red liquid sloshing in the bottom. "Sounds like you could use it."

Julien shook his head. "I couldn't. Madame Marchon would have something to say about that."

"Then don't tell her." She straightened up and pulled a strand of her loose silken hair behind her shoulder. "Besides, she knows I'm more than able to take care of myself."

Even in the moonlight Zéolie could see the blush that covered Julien's face. "I—I'd never give you any reason to—" he stammered.

Zéolie laughed and shook her head. "I know, Monsieur Haydel. Now, Julien, can we put the formalities aside and just be friends having a chat and a glass of wine?"

The young man on the street laughed and nodded.

"Lucien?" Zéolie called over her shoulder. Her hair swept over the railing. Far from the usual intricate coiffes of the French elite, Zéolie's loose waves were casual and enticing. Thoughts he couldn't afford to have flashed through his mind before being shoved aside.

"Lucien?" she called again.

From somewhere deep inside the house, a rich Creole voice answered, "Yes'm?"

"Would you please let Monsieur Haydel in and show him to the balcony?" Another 'yes'm' from the voice in the house as Zéolie settled herself on the chair to wait for her guest.

She knew the man Madame Marchon brought in to help around the house wouldn't say anything about her inviting a young gentleman to have a glass of wine on her balcony. Lucien was being paid well and wouldn't risk that, no matter what he may be thinking. He, like others, could hardly bring himself to look her in the eye even though she had been nothing but gentle with her new help. Rumors flew through the Quarter about Zéolie's death and resurrection, embellished heavily in the gossip of house servants. This made Zéolie an enigma of kindness and mystery that Lucien wasn't willing to challenge.

She toyed with the tarot cards on the small table next to her as she waited, picking the cards up and letting them dribble back down onto the deck. They were pliable and glistening in the evening humidity, sticking together enough that they were difficult to shuffle. When she was watching Julien grumbling his way down Dauphine Street, she had mixed them by hand, feeling their edges, letting them slide from one hand to the other. Now, they were an outlet for a fleeting wave of nerves.

"Michie Haydel." The deep resonance in Lucien's voice announced her guest as he was shown through Julien Cheval's study and onto the balcony. To some, the familiar form of 'monsieur' was crass, but Zéolie always loved it. With a warning glance at the young man, Lucien vanished into the house, but Zéolie knew he would stay close.

Julien stepped out onto the wooden planks of the balcony as though they were coated in ice, unsure of his own feet. Whatever courage he managed to muster the last time he was in her house had vanished.

Zéolie curled the corner of her mouth into a mischievous grin. "Don't tell me this is the first time you've sat in the dark with a girl?"

"No—I mean, I haven't— I—" Julien blushed and laughed. "I

don't make a habit of it," he said, regaining what little dignity he could salvage.

"I imagine your aunt wouldn't approve."

"No more than Lucien does."

Zéolie laughed and poured Julien a glass of wine, draining the bottle. "Maybe not as liberating as brandy, but it's delicious."

He settled himself into the chair opposite her and stretched his long legs out in front of him, crossing them at the ankle. As he let his self-consciousness slowly dissolve in the glass of wine, Zéolie's eyes traveled over him. Somewhere in all of his mother-hunting, he'd managed to work in a trip to the tailor. "I see you've traded your Paris fashion for something a bit more practical," she said over the rim of her wine glass.

"But still fashionable. Just not so damned hot."

"I'm sure Monsieur Gaspard was thrilled to replace your French clothes with his own creations."

Julien laughed. "To say the least. The man was giddy."

Zéolie laughed with him and shook her head. "No, that's just him all the time. Giddy as a schoolgirl when it comes to the cut of a waistcoat."

"To be honest, he talked me into more than I intended. I only went in there to see if he'd happened to make anything for my mother. One look at my trousers and, suddenly, he was a whirlwind of measuring tape and pins."

"Did you at least get a good lead out of it?"

Julien shook his dark head. "No, not a one."

Zéolie's brow wrinkled. "You'd think she'd make herself a little easier to find if she sent for you. And it's not just that. Even if something had happened to her where she couldn't be found, someone should know something, right? It's as though Marie Haydel never existed!"

Julien pulled his legs in and leaned forward on his knees. "I had the same thought. Someone should know something. No one even recognizes the name, but just to be sure, I sent word to the hospitals to see if she was there or ever had been. Nothing. A dead end." His young face took on years of weariness as he talked. His fruitless search for the mother he hoped to connect with after a lifetime of alienation was taking its toll. "Hell, I can't even describe the woman. I was a little boy the last time I saw her. Useless."

Zéolie threw back the end of her wine and sighed, letting the glass dangle between her fingers. "You need to take your mind off all this. Running yourself into the ground searching won't do you any good."

Fingers of her empty hand found the deck on the table. The cards. A thought swirled around in her mind, seductive and danger-ous. Risky if she didn't play it off just right. A way to get the informa-tion Julien needed hidden behind a taboo parlor game. Her hand hovered over the cards and energy tingled in her fingertips. She forced a grin as casually as she could, then lifted the deck into her hands, mixing them again. "On rainy nights, when there was nothing else to do, Celeste, Lisette, and I used to tell each other's fortunes. Silly stuff, but it was fun and took our minds off the gloominess."

"Something my aunt would disapprove of as much as sitting in the dark with a pretty girl." Julien chuckled.

Zéolie felt her cheeks warm. "Then, we're in a lot of trouble." *Even more if you knew what I'm doing,* she thought. Zéolie handed the deck to Julien. "Shuffle them. They're a little damp from being out here in the mugginess, so just mix them as best you can."

While he shuffled, Zéolie moved the small side table between them, setting the empty wine bottle and her glass on the balcony floor. Then, she took her place across the table.

"You need a scarf and some bracelets that jangle as you deal the cards," Julien said, placing the deck in her open palm.

"What?" Zéolie asked.

"Like the Paris gypsies. My cousin and I snuck into one of their shows once when we were young. There was an old lady in a tent with a scarf wrapped around her head, bracelets halfway up her arms, and a mole on the side of her nose."

Zéolie laughed. "You remember the mole after all these years?"

"More than the fortune. I have no idea what she told me. I was too busy trying to figure out how it didn't drive her crazy looking down her nose at that thing all the time!" Julien crossed his eyes and snorted.

"Well, then," Zéolie said, "let's see if I can tell your fortune without distracting you too much."

Julien knew that was as likely as him finding his mother in the morning. Zéolie might not have a mole on the side of her nose, but she was as distracting as that old gypsy. Captivating, beautiful, and distracting. Seduction without intending it. The curve of her cheek. The lilt of her laugh.

Cards shuffled and settled into their places in the deck as her hands worked them back and forth. "Should we ask them the obvious question?" Zéolie asked.

"You mean, where the hell is my mother?" Julien asked.

"That's the one."

The young man shook his head. "No, let's leave her out of it. I'm supposed to be getting my mind off things, right? You pick the question."

Thoughts she knew she should be running from pushed against her better judgement to the front of her mind. Ruthless in their tenacity, but careless. Intrusive. Things she could easily find out but had no business knowing. Better to play it safe. "How about a general past, present, and future spread?" she asked, forcing the other questions back where they belonged.

"Brace yourself. The past and present have been, well, odd. No telling what you'll see in those cards."

I'm counting on it. She may have picked a benign enough spread, but her own thoughts were aimed carefully at what she wanted to learn. Energy pooled in her palms as they held the cards, pouring her intentions into the deck, asking the questions he wouldn't.

Turning the top card of the deck over, she laid it on the table in front of her, the corner clicking against the tabletop as she pulled her finger away. "The ten of swords. Your past." Eight curved swords woven at the hilts with two in front, crossed at the points. The corner of her mouth curled as she looked up at Julien. "Usually I'd hesitate to tell you about this one, but it's nothing new to you. Affliction, hidden pain." Julien chuckled uncomfortably and Zéolie forced a smile. Those things were true, but not the only thing in the card. Mental instability. Insanity. She'd left it out to protect Julien from what she feared for him. If the card was right, this mother of his that he was desperate to find wasn't what he thought she was.

"You didn't need a card to figure that out," Julien said. His fingers found his watch chain and twisted it.

"I said I'd *tell* your fortune, not change it."

"Fair enough." His fingers let the watch chain dangle again. "So, we've got my childhood covered. Now what?"

Another click of the corner of a card and Zéolie's hand froze for an instant before pulling back. Fingers wrapped the deck tightly to keep from trembling. Her voice caught in her throat, wanting nothing to do with the words. "The Hanged Man. Your present." Once again, the smirking figure dangling by his ankle looked up at her. Her breath came shallow and fast. The card that started it all. This was no coincidence.

"What does it mean?" Julien asked. He wasn't looking at the man on the card, grinning with his legs in the shape of the number four, hanging there as if it were perfectly normal. Instead, Julien's attention was on Zéolie and the blue lines streaking across her face that had gone suddenly pale. In the flickering lamplight, he could have sworn she flinched. If this was just fun and games, why was she frightened?

"Sacrifice, martyrdom, detachment," she managed to choke out.

Julien watched her face intently as she struggled to keep control of something. That wasn't so bad. What was scaring her so much? "Sounds right. I'm about as detached from my mother and home as I could ever be. And I've sacrificed more time and money on this than any sane person would."

Zéolie pulled herself together and shook the weight of the past from her shoulders. It didn't go willingly. Rather, it slid slowly off her like a thick slime, coating her in doubt and foreboding. "True," she answered. "I guess that one wasn't helpful either."

"He's a strange little man hanging upside down like that. And happy enough about it. Can't be too bad."

You have no idea. "No, I guess not. And not much of a revelation."

"One more?" Julien asked, assuming there was a third for his future.

Zéolie nodded and turned the last card over. Her breath caught sharply in her chest, settling there in a dead weight. On the table, two men fell from a crumbling, flaming tower. She scanned her memory of the card meanings searching for anything about this card that could be positive. "The Tower. Your future."

Julien said. "It doesn't look good."

"The cards don't always show us what will be. Sometimes, it's a warning of what *could* be. Especially with the future card."

Julien picked up the card and held it to the light from the study streaming through the windows. As he turned the card, the falling figures seemed to tumble, stopping just short of smashing to the ground. "I'm going to take a guess that it doesn't mean I'm going to fall off a big building."

Zéolie tried to laugh. "No. The cards aren't ever literal. Don't go climbing the cathedral, though. Just in case," Zéolie said, forcing any levity she could muster into her words. Either she danced around what she was seeing in the cards and give him some candy-coated version of the meaning or tell him what she really saw. Deciding her handsome young guest had been through enough bad news, she decided to hedge the truth like she did with Lisette. "Change. It means a change is coming. Maybe not one you expect." Close enough. 'Tumultuous upheaval' watered down to 'unexpected change.'

Julien watched her face as he tapped the card on his fingertips. The blue lines had deepened, and shadows were draped under her eyes. Rumors had found their way to his ears, and he knew that even if a fraction of it was true, it was enough to make Zéolie easily worn out. Julien wanted to think she was just tired, but there was something more. Her eyes weren't slow moving and drooping with sleep. They were darting and distant. Fear. What was she hiding and why?

As much as he wanted to know, he couldn't bring himself to press her. Tossing the card on the table, he said, "Well, that last one definitely got my mind off things." Julien picked up his glass and went to take another sip of wine but found the glass had run dry. Shrugging, he set it down on the table next to the swords, tower, and hanging man. "It's late and I've intruded long enough. I should go."

"Not running away from a few playing cards, are you?" Zéolie teased, trying to lighten an atmosphere that had gone leaden.

Julien grinned. His smile flirted with hers before becoming serious. "Not at all. It was fun. But it's late and I'm sure Lucien wants to go to bed. God knows he's not going to budge from that threshold until I'm gone."

Zéolie looked through the tall windowpanes into her father's study and saw the subtle movement of a dark shadow in the hallway door. Lucien stayed out of ear shot so he wouldn't be accused of eavesdropping, but close enough to make sure he was there should Julien lose his gentility. "I wish Alida would take her cleaning duties as seriously as he takes his chaperoning."

Her young guest stood and stretched his back. "Better not give him any reason to tattle to Madame Marchon. Although, that might be more fun than the intimidating cards." He took Zéolie's outstretched hand and lightly kissed it, like a perfect gentleman. What Lucien didn't see was Julien's wink as he raised his head and let go of her hand.

Before she could catch herself, she winked back.

Moments later, she was giving a wave over the railing to a tall slender shadow before it vanished into the New Orleans fog. As his footsteps faded, muffled by the mist, her eyes settled on the cards. Doubt and fear bobbed to the surface from the depths she had pushed them. Zéolie wasn't finished, and it had something to do with Julien Haydel.

TEN

No matter how hard Julien tried to focus on his elusive mother, he inevitably found himself pulled into Zéolie's orbit. There was a comfort in her presence as she talked him through dead ends and missing pieces in his search. More than that, she was holding more of his young heart each time he was with her. Never flirting like Celeste, Zéolie was warm, familiar, and strong. Emotions churned in his chest, threatening to reveal themselves despite his efforts at casual friendship.

Once more, he found himself in the parlor of the house on Dauphine along with the Marchon girls who seemed to be there more often than not. "Monsieur Vidal seemed to recognize her name at first, but then realized he, like everyone else, was thinking of the family on the plantation."

Zéolie leaned back in her chair and toyed with a loose thread on her skirt. "I know I've asked you this before, Julien, but really think. Did your mother ever mention the plantation?"

Celeste sashayed past a bowl of fruit and plucked a grape from the bunch. "We've been through this already." She popped the grape into her mouth and draped herself across the settee.

"I know," Zéolie said. "There just has to be some connection. The name isn't that common in the city."

Julien shook his head. "She hasn't mentioned much of anything in her letters. And my aunt said even less. I wish the old bat would've told me something. Anything! Uncle would have, if he'd been around." He got up and paced infrustration. "Aunt Regina was too busy spending hours shoving her gray hair under wigs styled like next season's debutantes and rubbing rouge on her wrinkled cheeks. She's got a good heart, but compassion takes a backseat to fashion."

Something didn't sit right with Zéolie. "Gray hair and wrinkles? How much older than your mother is your aunt?"

"A lot. She's my great-aunt. That's just too much to say all the time, and since she raised me, she never felt as distant as that sounds."

"If she wasn't a sibling, did she ever say if your mother had a brother or sister?" As the question left her lips, Zéolie felt a pull in her palms. Energy collected there, pulsing. She was onto something, but she couldn't figure out what.

"She never mentioned anyone. When I was little and first got to Paris, my aunt and uncle used to talk in front of me thinking I wasn't listening or was too young to understand. There were other names when they talked about her. But I never heard them again once Uncle went away."

"Away?" Lisette asked. She had been so quiet they almost forgot she was there.

Julien smiled at her and Lisette blushed deep red. "My uncle was —colorful. Out of everyone in that mausoleum, Uncle Faron was the most fun. At first, it was little things, like letting doves fly around the house. I never knew where he got them or where they went later. They were just there, flying around. He did it all the time to entertain me, until one left something in the middle of the foyer floor. Aunt Regina was furious. She didn't need the rouge that day." Julien grinned at Lisette who dissolved into a puddle of shyness.

"She didn't send him away over dove droppings, did she?"

Celeste asked, taking far more interest in the mischievous uncle than the pompous aunt.

His dark eyes twinkled. "Not the doves, no. I believe it had more to do with the late-night roaming and babbling about what he would do to her "pompous bouffant" if she didn't let him be whatever the hell he wanted to be. Who knows what he was talking about, but she wasn't ever one to back down. The last time I saw him, he walked into the night smoking a cigar while doctors made sure the flames in Regina's wig hadn't scorched her scalp."

"Good god!" Zéolie said louder than she meant to.

Keeping a safe distance from Celeste and her wandering hands, Julien sat next to Zéolie. Heat rose in his chest, relishing the closeness to her, but mocking him as it danced on the edges of his good sense. "I always tried to imagine how he did it. There was some yelling and a screech, then chaos. From my room, I could hear it all, but never knew exactly what was going on. There was some heated talking, a shriek, then Regina came tearing out of her room holding her flaming wig in front of her on the end of the brass poker from her bedroom fireplace. By then, I'd come out to see what was going on, just in time to see Uncle Faron wink at me, light a cigar, and stroll out into the night. I never saw him again."

She couldn't explain why, but Zéolie could see the scene playing out in front of her. A film of haze blurred the details, but she could definitely see it. She wanted to search the vision and move around in it, but she was chained to whatever memory Julien had created of the event. But why could she see it at all when she wasn't even trying?

"Sounds violent," Lisette muttered.

"I don't think it was. The doctors asked if he'd attacked her. Regina yelled at them and insisted that was a ridiculous thing to say. She never did say how he did it. I thought he'd just tossed it into the fire grate, but there was nothing burning in there that night. Never did figure that one out."

"Did your aunt ever hear from him?" Celeste asked, too fascinated by the uncle to remember to flirt.

"Not that I know of." Julien's long legs stretched out, relaxing into his story. "I used to tell myself he went off to become a pirate. Anyone who could take on Aunt Regina and walk away like that could take on any ruler of the high seas. I know it's ridiculous, but it just seemed like something he'd do. Of course, Aunt Regina said he should've been locked up with Uncle Jacques in the asylum."

"Uncle Jacques? Her brother?" Zéolie asked.

"Sorry, I'm not doing a good job keeping the family tree straight. No, Jacques was married to Faron's sister. Uncle by marriage. Complicated stuff."

Something deep inside Zéolie sizzled. She was getting closer. But closer to what?

Celeste laughed, cutting off Zéolie's next question, which was probably a good thing. Zéolie had to be careful with her curiosity. There were enough questions churning in her for a full interrogation, but if she wasn't careful, he'd start to wonder about her sudden interest.

"Sounds like the women in your family have interesting taste in men," Celeste said coyly.

"Or the interesting men in my family have boring taste in women," Julien said winking at her. "I hope I manage to be the exception to the rule."

That last sentence was directed at Zéolie. As sweet as it was, the compliment didn't go down easy. It soured in her ears. Any time Julien said something that smacked of seriousness about her, Louis' face was in front of hers, jealous and hurt. "Sounds like your Uncle Jacques might have been the more interesting one."

Julien laughed. "I wouldn't know. He was dead long before I was born. But the stories about him were less of the spirited adventurer like Fernand and more of a raving lunatic."

Lisette's soft voice piped up from the window seat. "How did he die? Ja—Jacques, I mean. How did he die?"

"Leave it to Lisette to turn a funny story into something morbid," Celeste said, rolling her eyes at her sister.

"Sorry, I didn't mean—" Lisette's amber eyes teared up as she tried to hide her embarrassment.

"It's alright," Julien said gently. "But Celeste has a point. That's a morbid one. He hung himself."

An invisible weight slammed into Zéolie's chest almost knocking her off the chair. Trying desperately to hide what was going on inside her, she stood up and rang for Lucien. "Maybe something to eat and a game of cards will lighten things up," she said, bringing Julien's tale to a halt. There was no doubt in her mind that Julien's family history was somehow tied to what she was supposed to do, and Camille was making sure she noticed.

Fighting against the onslaught of energy from her grandmother was wearing on her. As she reached for the bell on the desk, she could see the blue veins streaking up her arms and knew they were weaving across her face as well.

Lucien appeared almost instantly, never being far away when Julien visited. "Yes'm?" he asked. Taking one look at the strain and veins, he added softly, "Tea?" Zéolie nodded.

The tea was a necessity but kept secret out of safety for Zéolie. The fewer people who knew what was giving her strength, the safer she was. Lucien, Zéolie, and Mother Micheaux were the only ones who knew. Even Lucien and Zéolie didn't know how it was made. That secret resided with Mother Micheaux.

"Some refreshments would be nice, Lucien. Small plates. We'll play cards while we eat," Zéolie directed. "I'll have something for you to deliver when you return." Lucien nodded and glanced over at Julien before he left to carry out her orders. She knew he didn't like being across the courtyard with a young man in a parlor full of women.

"Oh!" Celeste said snapping her fingers. "We can plan your party while we play!" she said with a grin at Julien.

"Party?" Lisette asked.

Celeste ran a finger across Julien's shoulders as she passed behind him. "Our boy is becoming a man," she teased. "Twenty-one next week."

An electric pulse raced down Zéolie's spine. Twenty-one. The night her world shattered. Power flooded her body threatening to burst through her hands. *Not now, Camille!* Curling her fingers, she dug her nails into her palm to get control. The echo of her mother's laugh rang in her ears. Deep, distant, and haunting.

The Marchon girls and Julien cleared a small table and pulled chairs around it while Zéolie sat at her desk dashing off a note to Mother Micheaux.

There's someone you need to meet. But first, we need to talk. Midday? Z.

Camille had something to say, and they were going to be ready for her.

CHAPTER

ELEVEN

S leep flirted with Julien but left him restless. Zéolie's face occupied his waking hours, smiling and gentle. Often, she found her way into his dreams, too, but his nights were slowly being consumed with nightmares. Flashes of terrifying images that he couldn't place. Nothing from his own life. Faces he didn't know. Raging or terrified. Most of the images were so fast he couldn't see them clearly, but the sensations lingered. Fear. Anger. Power. Sometimes he saw himself stepping gingerly through a sleeping boggy wood, then choking and gagging as the burning trees around him hissed. A sliver of moonlight, then a flash of lightning. None of it made sense.

Night after night, it wore on. Each morning, he woke more exhausted, and somehow feeling it had to do with the search for his mother. Or the search was wearing him down and causing the dreams. One seemed as likely as the other at this point.

Maybe he'd spent too much time in a strange place, but he felt different in New Orleans. Stronger. Independent. Intuitive. The last one surprised him the most. Knowing without a doubt when someone was lying to him, confused, or genuinely glad to see him, all going beyond basic body language and signals. Even more than that, he knew what they were thinking. Not specifics, but generalizations. Most people's thoughts were an open book, no matter how hard they tried to hide behind their overbred manners, but not everyone.

One person was decidedly out of reach of his new intuition. Zéolie. It was as though other people had a transparency to them, but she was solid rock. Warm and welcoming on the surface, but a fortress mentally and emotionally. Celeste's thoughts were wanton and open, tempting and embarrassing at the same time. She had a warmth and playfulness that he sometimes found himself swept up by. Lisette's were innocent and shy, but kind and nurturing. Their mother was loving toward the girls, but guarded with others, especially him. Julien could understand that. He was a stranger in the city and her daughter was throwing herself at him any chance she got. If Madame Marchon knew what was going on inside Celeste's head, the girl would find herself in the Ursuline convent by sundown.

Running out of leads in his search for his mother, Julien began to entertain himself in the city. His mother had been elusive as long as he could remember, which made it easy to let the urgency fade. New Orleans was intoxicating. Paris was more refined, ornate, and cultured. There was a wildness about New Orleans, in spite of the attempts of the French to civilize it. It was loose around the edges that bled into the depths of sultry swamps. The roughness of the riverfront frayed unapologetically into the manners of the deep Quarter. As alien as it was to the only life he could remember, Julien Haydel had never felt more at home.

Part of that he owed to Zéolie. She welcomed him, entertained him, and served as a sounding board for his frustrations. There was a small part of Julien that thought of giving up on this whole search for a woman who wouldn't be found and going back to Paris. Every time that thought entered his mind, it was dashed quickly to the ground by his fascination with Zéolie Cheval. In his naivete, he imagined his having the same name as the father she lost as a soul connection. Her address being the one his mother led him to, he saw as no accident. Julien's mind raced when he was with her, knowing she was out of reach but wanting her anyway. Heart fluttering, gut twisting thoughts. The worst part, though, was that he was certain Zéolie knew it, even though he had done his best to hide it. Somehow, she knew. If he was right, and Zéolie did know how he felt about her, she couldn't feel the same for him. She'd never done anything to lead him on, except one wink after a night of wine and conversation. He clung to that as hope there was more.

Everything about her wasn't charm and romance. There was something she was hiding. Something that occupied her thoughts and frightened her. Part of him attributed it to whatever she'd gone through to spawn ridiculous rumors in the Quarter, but he knew there was more to it. He couldn't read Zéolie like the others, but he watched her so intently that flickers in her expression were enough for him to know there was something lurking under the surface of her impenetrable facade. Julien could only imagine what could shake the foundation of someone so in control. Whatever it was, he wished she would tell him. Julien may not be able to rescue her from it, but he wanted to help. He owed her that much. Somewhere, inside her fortress, Zéolie was at war.

Closing his eyes, focused on her laugh over a losing hand of cards, he willed his dreams to be filled with her instead of the raging nightmares.

MOTHER MICHEAUX CROUCHED in the courtyard garden in a puddle of black cloth. Her hands nimbly plucked leaves from plants needed to brew Zéolie's swamp tea and dropped them in the tiny basket. As she did, their aromas, earthy and rich, hung in the stagnant air. On the other side of the zodiac wheel of herbs and flowers, Zéolie paced. "How much longer will I need the tea?" she asked.

"As long as it takes."

"Don't you know how long that could be?" Zéolie asked impatiently.

The mother superior looked up from her work leveling her gaze at Zéolie. "I've never done this before. Resurrection is usually reserved for a higher power. One who would have a better answer for you."

Zéolie stopped pacing and dropped her eyes. "Sorry. I shouldn't have said that."

"Why don't you tell me what's really on your mind? I know you didn't ask me here to do gardening." The old nun stood slowly, arched her back, and dusted her hands on her habit. "Maybe over a nice cup of tea?"

Zéolie groaned and rolled her eyes. "If only I had a nice cup of tea. I'll tell you over swamp water."

"Fair enough," the mother superior laughed.

∽

"Now," Mother Micheaux said blowing across the top of her cup, "you have some explaining to do."

Zéolie held her breath and took a gulp of the disgusting herbal concoction, screwing her face up as it stung down her throat. "Ugh. I'll never get used to that," she muttered.

"You don't really have a choice. Now, tell me about Julien Haydel." The old nun's face was relaxed but her words were cold.

Zéolie almost spit swamp water tea into her lap. "You know?"

"Some. Madame Marchon mentioned him. Seems her girls are pretty taken with the young man."

Laughing, Zéolie said, "I should say so! Lisette can't form a coherent sentence around him and Celeste couldn't be more obvious in throwing herself at Julien if she stripped down to her skivvies."

Mother Micheaux tsked and blew on her coffee. "I see. And this is who you wanted me to meet?"

Zéolie nodded and choked down another swallow of nastiness. "How much did Madame Marchon tell you about Julien?"

"Aside from the girls, not much. He's in town looking for his mother and happened to have your house as the wrong address. You and the girls were kind to him, but useless in his search. He doesn't really know anyone else in town, so he spends time here with you and the Marchons."

Zéolie expected the nun to pass judgement on her keeping company with a young man and was surprised when she didn't. She'd given no reason for anyone to question her propriety, which likely mollified Mother Micheaux, especially with Lucien charged by Madame Marchon to keep watch over Zéolie. "Then you know the gist." She absently tapped her finger on the edge of her cup.

"And?" Mother Micheaux asked.

"And," Zéolie sighed, "I think he has something to do with Camille."

Mother Micheaux's eyes narrowed, then relaxed again. "How do you mean?"

"There are...signals from her. I guess that's the right word. She's trying to get my attention when he mentions certain things. Like I should know something I can't figure out."

"Such as?"

Zéolie told her about the night on the balcony and the tarot cards. The mother superior listened intently with little reaction until she mentioned the Hanged Man card. She knew what effect that had on Zéolie and, if Zéolie was right, that was no coincidence.

"He was talking about his family and there were times she's almost knocked the wind out of me. An uncle seemed to have most of her attention."

"Uncle? I thought it was the mother that was his big problem."

"She is, but it seems that he's given up on finding her. Can't blame him, really. The woman's not making this easy on him."

Mother Micheaux shook her head. "No. And if he didn't have a relationship with her from the start, it's easier to give up." Taking a slow sip of her coffee, she thought for a moment. "Tell me more about this uncle of his."

"Julien was raised by his great-aunt Regina who was married to Faron. He never said a last name."

"And you think Camille has an interest in Faron?" the nun asked.

Zéolie shook her head. "Not him." Sweat beaded on her top lip and her heart fluttered as the words swirled in her mind. They fought against her, not wanting to be heard, retreating and being pushed forward in a mental tug-of-war. Bracing herself in case Camille decided to react, slowly, she convinced the words to make their way to her lips. "Julien's great-uncle. Jacques."

As much as the mother superior wanted to breathe, she couldn't. Her chest refused to open. Finally, air came in sharp and shallow. It couldn't be. Surely not. "What do you know about him?" The question was hollow.

"Julien never met him. Jacques died long before he was born, so he only knew what his aunt said. She called her brother-in-law a raving lunatic." Electricity shot through Zéolie, fighting for her attention, searching for an outlet. Her face contorted as she tried to contain it. Every time Camille tugged at her, it got harder for her to keep under control. Hair on her skin stood on end and every cell tingled.

Mother Micheaux watched her transforming. Skin white, veins streaking even with the tea. Something had hold of the girl in an ever-tightening grip. She could only hope it was Camille. "Let it go," she whispered. "Release it. Safely."

Through clenched teeth, Zéolie asked, "How?"

The nun scanned the parlor for a suitable target. "The mantle."

Zéolie relaxed and held her palms out toward the mantle shelf. With her next breath, the brass candlesticks warmed and began to ooze over the edge and drip into the fireplace grate. Flowers in the vases lifted out and hovered above the mouths as cracks streaked across the surfaces of the glass in an intricate lace. Another breath and they burst in a swirl of glittering shards.

"Now, put them back," the mother superior ordered calmly.

Closing her eyes, Zéolie pulled her hands closer to her body, palms facing but not touching each other and the dancing splinters of glass began to reassemble and fuse together. Hot brass dripped upwards from the fireplace onto the mantle seeping back into the shapes of the candlesticks. Finally, the flower stems settled back into the vases and drooped sleepily. With the twitch of the last leaf, Zéolie relaxed.

"Better?" Mother Micheaux asked.

"For now. Camille has something to say," Zéolie said flatly.

The old nun nodded. "I know. But you can't let her take control of you. She'll get her say." Mother Micheaux uncurled fingers that had gone white gripping the coffee cup and set it down on the side table. "Shall we?" she asked with a nod to the covered basket hiding in plain sight in the corner of the room.

Zéolie was tired from controlling the energy in her veins, but knew she needed to give Camille a chance to speak if any of this was going to let up. "Let's do it." She stood, draining the last of the noxious tea, and went to pick up the basket. As she did, there was a knock on the door. The women locked eyes. "Damn!" Zéolie cursed. "I forgot."

"Expecting someone?" Mother Micheaux asked.

"Julien. Every day, like clockwork."

Mother Micheaux looked at her, suspecting there was more to Julien's attentiveness, but said nothing.

"Michie Julien," Lucien said, showing the young man in with a nod to the mother superior.

Julien strode into the room, straight for Zéolie, grinning. "You may need to have a talk with Celeste," he said reaching for her hand and kissing it. "I don't think her mother's going to approve of some of the things she has planned for the party. I mean, they sound like fun, but..." He trailed off as Mother Micheaux stood. "I—I'm sorry, Mother. I—I didn't see you there."

"It's alright. I don't believe we've met. You must be Julien."

His face colored as he took her hand. "Julien Haydel."

Zéolie watched the nun's face for any sign of disapproval or flashes of intuition about his family connections, but there was no expression beyond simple politeness. *Nothing. No reaction. She must be hell at a card table.*

"Zéolie tells me you've been looking for your mother," the nun said. "Any luck?"

Julien shook his dark head and pushed his fingers through his hair. "Not yet. Honestly, I doubt I will. She doesn't seem to want to be found."

Mother Micheaux folded her hands at her waist. Zéolie knew that stance. Outward reverence, inward strength. She was on guard. "Perhaps," the nun said, "she doesn't know what she's missing. Her handsome son seems to have done well for himself. I'm sure if she could see you now, she'd be proud." It was politeness and patronization. Generic. Her words were stagnant, but her eyes were sharp, traveling over him taking in every detail before settling on his eyes.

Julien shifted uncomfortably under her scrutiny. Mentally, he reached out trying to understand the meaning behind her blank words, but there was nothing. Like Zéolie, Mother Micheaux was a fortress. He expected judgement, religious fervor, anything. He got nothing.

"Y—yes," he stammered. "I'm sure she would. Thank you."

The mother superior's mouth smiled, but it didn't travel to her eyes. "Zéolie also tells me you've become quite a fixture around here."

Julien glanced at Zéolie and his expression softened. "She's been kind enough to welcome me and offer help where she can. Unfortunately, I'm afraid I've given her a headache over the whole thing." The young man smiled warmly at the beauty next to him.

Zéolie smiled back. "Nonsense. Who doesn't love a good mystery?"

He shrugged. "Me. I've had quite enough of chasing shadows and phantoms. If she wants to see me, she can come looking for me for a change."

"Wise, too, I see," Mother Micheaux said. "Often, if we can't find a solution, we need to step back and let the solution find us." The nun glanced at Zéolie, whose warmth toward the boy wasn't lost on her, then back to Julien. "I do wish we could visit longer, Monsieur Haydel, but Zéolie and I were on our way out and we really shouldn't be late."

Zéolie shot the nun a look of sheer confusion but knew better than to question the mother superior. "I'm sorry, Julien," she said recovering her poise. "She's right. But I'll talk to Celeste for you, not that it'll do any good."

"It's worth a try!" Julien said with a laugh. "I won't keep you," he said to Zéolie. To the mother superior: "It was a pleasure. I hope we'll meet again." With a bow to both women, he showed himself out.

As soon as the door closed behind him, Zéolie wheeled around on the old nun. "What was that about? I know you're anxious to hear from Camille, but we didn't have to run him off."

Mother Micheaux looked squarely at Zéolie. "There's something you need to see."

CHAPTER

TWELVE

Mother Micheaux was stoic on the carriage ride to the Ursuline convent, pretending to lose herself in prayers that wouldn't come. Zéolie knew the prayers weren't there, but let the nun have time in her own mind. Whatever the mother superior needed her to see, she'd find out soon enough.

The carriage set them down in front of one of the rear entrances to the convent. With a nod to the driver, Mother Micheaux pulled a key from her skirt and slid it into the iron lock. Metal hissed softly as the bolt slid back and settled into its berth. The heavy wooden door swung silently open on hinges dripping with fresh oil. Great care had been taken to make sure any entrance through this door was virtually undetectable.

But why does the mother superior need to sneak into her own convent? Zéolie wondered.

Mother Micheaux opened the door just wide enough for her and Zéolie to slip through before silently closing it again. Metal hissed again as the bolt barred the door once more. Darkness draped itself heavily over them as the light of the afternoon was banished to the outside. Even as her eyes adjusted, Zéolie realized the corridor was only lit at the far end by a gas lamp turned almost completely down. Only a faint shimmer of light guided their steps. Even in the dark, Zéolie knew this place. She could smell the damp mustiness and staleness of the unused passageway. The last time she was here, she was heading out the door they just came in, hoping never to return. Blood drained from her face as she realized whatever she was here to see was in the stone room under the convent. *What the hell is this woman hiding now?*

The mother superior walked ahead, mouthing words that should have been prayers, but instead were incantations. One by one lifting protections and curses as they passed through the long hallway, then replacing each one behind them. A small blue flame glowed on a shallow table against the wall at the top of the stairs that only barely illuminated the change in level of the floor. Mother Micheaux didn't really need it. Her feet had found these steps enough times to know the way on their own.

Zéolie followed her wordlessly into the inky blackness of the stairs where the light refused to follow. Her hand running along the wall beside her felt the change from rippled plaster to hard stone as they descended into the damp depths beneath the convent. Whispered steps of the mother superior stopped in front of her as they reached the bottom. Fabric rustled. Iron grated on iron. Hinges creaked softly. A wave of rich earthiness washed over them on the warm lamplight.

The room Zéolie knew too well had transformed. It still had the same slick, lichen-covered walls and earthen floor, but the room was now filled with all sorts of magical things. Bottles in all sizes with strange mixtures inside lined wooden shelves. Bunches of herbs hung upside down from the low ceiling. Candle stumps and tools surrounded by trinkets, small bones, and pottery cups littered the large table in the center.

As she surveyed the room, a figure stepped slowly out of the shadow in the corner, with movements like liquid grace. Scarves seemed to float loosely around the woman's waist in stark contrast to the tignon wound tightly around her head. Moss green eyes set in caramel skin settled on Zéolie's face.

Zéolie staggered backwards several steps as she took in the woman standing in front of her. Words surged but got lost on the way to her mouth that was opening and closing noiselessly. Color drained from her cheeks and veins streaked like a map across her face. Her breath came fast and shallow as the woman reached out for her. Blood pounded in her ears. She saw the woman move her mouth to say something but couldn't hear her. Blackness gathered at the edges of her vision as she sank into oblivion.

A HAND WAS under her head holding it up as another hand dribbled water into her mouth. Sputtering, Zéolie opened her eyes. Above her, white teeth shone between burgundy lips that smiled down at her. Mossy eyes danced and winked. "Guess we should'a had ya sit down first," the woman laughed.

Zéolie squinted up at the face silhouetted above her. "Mama Nell?" she whispered. The woman nodded. "But-how? I—you were *dead.*"

Mama Nell chuckled. "Now, child, you should know that doesn't mean much these days." She put her cool hand on Zéolie's forehead. "Besides, you can't get rid of me that easy. There's work to do."

"But I saw it," Zéolie said, struggling to sit up on the floor. "I—I *did* it."

Mama Nell sat down on the ground next to Zéolie and curled her feet up under her skirt. She took one of Zéolie's pale hands in hers. "I never got the chance to tell you about the ones that look after us. Especially those of us who work their magic. You see, *chérie*, jus' like you, I had ancestors who knew I wasn't finished. Magic misfires, 'specially when we're learnin'. I don't put all those protection spells aroun' me for nothin'." Mama Nell squeezed her hand. "Now, let's try this again." She held out her arms. Bracelets clinked softly. "It's good to see you, child."

With tears streaming down her face, Zéolie fell into the embrace, letting the warmth of her aunt wash over her. Pain and relief collided in her chest and poured from her eyes in wracking sobs. The priestess stroked her hair and let her cry, rocking her gently until her breathing settled and the tears began to ebb.

Zéolie looked up at her with bloodshot eyes. "If you've been alive all this time, why didn't you tell me? Where have you been?"

Mother Micheaux answered for her, "Helping me."

"I—I don't understand."

Mama Nell patted her hand. "I know." She glanced up at the mother superior. "Think she can handle it?"

The nun shrugged. "She's going to have to. We need her."

The priestess nodded and stood in one liquid movement. Holding out her hand, she brought Zéolie to her feet. Confusion was splashed across the girl's face as Nell led her to the far side of the room that was shrouded in darkness. A sheet was draped over a rope anchored in the stone, creating a makeshift curtain across the corner. Slowly, Mama Nell drew the curtain back.

Lamplight pierced the darkness and tumbled in shadows across the figure laying on the cot. Curls wet with perspiration smeared across his forehead. On his chest was an angry scar. Down his arms were raised red scars of the witch's sigils her mother had carved there. Zéolie's heart jumped into her throat.

"Louis!" She choked on the words as sobs shook her. Gripping the stone wall, she fought to keep her feet. Her tear-filled eyes took all of him in. He'd been through hell, but he was alive. As a thought struck her, she turned on the mother superior. "You told me you didn't know what happened to him? Why didn't you tell me he was alive?" she snarled with too many emotions at once.

The nun held out her hand to block any magical misfire as the girl in front of her raged. "Zéolie, please listen to me. We struggled bringing him back. When you asked me that, I didn't want to tell you he was alive only to lose him again if he slipped away from us. He's been harder to bring back."

"Why?"

"Besides not having a witch on the other side to push him back, or his own witch's strength to pull himself back, he's fought us."

"Fought you? Why would he do that?"

"See for yourself." The nun waved her hand toward Louis' body.

Zéolie took a step toward the cot and looked at Mama Nell, who nodded. Standing over his bed, the torture was even more shocking. Sweat beaded on his forehead and trickled down his temples into his curls. Whiskers covered his once smooth jaw, kept trimmed, she assumed, by Mama Nell. Under closed eyelids, his eyes darted frantically with tormented sleep.

Zéolie's hand hovered over his forehead for a moment before she let it lower to touch him. As she did, her mind was flooded with images and sensations. Memories of Louis' struggle against her mother. Solène's voice rang through her ears and she almost jerked her hand back. Cackling, raging, chaos. Inside his memory, invisible hands clawed at her body and ran through her hair turning her stomach as she realized what her mother had done the night she tricked Louis into racing to the cabin in the swamp.

Zéolie's own anger threatened to pull her out of Louis' mind as she fought to control her emotions. Pushing her hatred aside, she let herself sink deeper into his thoughts.

"Louis?" she called softly. "Can you hear me?" Thoughts that had been clear began to cloud into a haze. "Louis, please let me in. I want to help you, but you need to let me see what you're fighting." Her pleading seemed to have some effect as the thoughts became clearer.

Seeing through his eyes, she was face to face with herself. She was pleading with him, but he was resisting. Her mother raged and danced on the rooftop behind her as the trees burned. Smoke stung Louis' eyes as tears of grief gathered there. Louis knew what he had to do. There was no way around it, no matter how much his logical mind searched for another answer. The only way to destroy the witch was to destroy the one thing she wanted.

Zéolie watched and remembered with him as his hand took the silver blade from her hand and curled his fingers around it. Louis pulled her close, kissing her. *Forgive me, Zéolie*, he thought as he slid the blade between her ribs into her heart. Bile rose in the back of his throat, burning as he looked down at the life draining from her body. Red precious life spilling from the knife he had driven into her heart. She smiled at him as her skin went ashen and she stumbled back from him. "I love you, Louis." she whispered. "I am my own, now. *Je suis le mein.*"

"I love you, Zéolie. With all that I am. I love you. *Vous êtes votre propre, et je suis à toi.*" Louis said as lightning flashed around them.

Then, Zéolie finally saw what happened after her death. Her mother's rage turned on Louis as she pulled energy from the storm. Too much, Zéolie realized. Solène ignited in a wild burst of power and lightning. Through Louis' eyes, she watched her mother burn into oblivion as her skin bubbled and peeled away from her bones, writhing in agony and destruction on the crumbling rooftop.

Unable to bring himself to watch any more of the grotesque demise of the witch, he looked down at Zéolie. The world around him faded into shadows and echoes of reality as he looked at the face of the woman he loved. Firelight glinted on the intricate handle of the silver knife in her chest. Kneeling beside her, he kissed her cold lips as a sob choked him. Pain and guilt consumed Louis. She was gone and it was his fault. His hand drove the knife into her. He was the one who couldn't stop the witch without sacrificing Zéolie. He failed her when she needed him. He killed her.

Wrapping his hands around the knife, he slid it out of her body and turned it over in his hand. Her blood on the blade. Running his finger through the blood, he knew what he had to do. There was nothing left for him here. He didn't deserve to go on if she didn't. He kissed her cold lips goodbye and jammed the blade into his own chest.

"No, Louis!" Zéolie shrieked. "Oh, god, no! *No!*" She was thrown into swirling blackness then the memory started over on a hideous loop of agony and guilt. Yanking her hand from his forehead, she forced herself into her own painful reality and collapsed.

Moments later, she opened her eyes to find Mama Nell once more reviving her. "Sorry you had to go through that, *chérie*," her aunt said softly. "You needed to see it yourself to understan' what we're workin' against."

Zéolie looked over Mama Nell's shoulder at Mother Micheaux. "You said you needed my help. What can I do?"

"Nothing we've done can break through his own guilt. We have the strength to bring him back if he wants to come back, but you may be the key to him wanting to. Adding your strength to ours, and you convincing him to, we should be able to break through his barrier."

Zéolie nodded. "I'll help. He's suffered too much as it is."

Mother Micheaux nodded at Mama Nell. The priestess began lighting the candles and coal for burning incense, chanting ancient prayers as she worked. In a mortar and pestle, she began crushing herbs and mixing in oils to create a thick paste. Zéolie wondered how much of what her aunt was doing was to bring Louis back and how much was protection against Zéolie's inability to control her own magic.

THIRTEEN

Zéolie stood over Louis, watching his eyes twitch under closed lids, wondering what part of the horror he was reliving at that moment. On either side of her were Mama Nell and Mother Micheaux. Behind them, candles flickered and popped. Zéolie's face was drawn and pale, streaked with blue veins as the strain wore on her. She hoped she had enough strength to be what Louis needed her to be.

The mother superior raised her hands out in front of her in the same gesture she would have used to bless communion. Instead, she was calling a stranger power, or maybe the same power in different form, to her aid. Words that Zéolie had come to know poured from the nun's mouth where prayers should have been as her aging hands stretched over Louis' body.

Like a chorus in the round, Zéolie took up the chant after Mother Micheaux, followed by Mama Nell. An eerie chorus of angels fallen from grace calling on the only powers that could help them now. Their voices rang off the damp stone walls and echoed around them. Alive in their magic, the words swirled high and low between them and wound together in a dance of strength and beauty. Three voices in harmony calling down all the power they could into the one who gave everything for the woman he loved.

As the last of the words rang in the air, Zéolie touched her hand to Louis' forehead. Memories rushed her, but she held her hand out, holding them at bay. "Enough," she snapped. "Enough of that. It's time, Louis." The onslaught of memories backed away and a haze took their place. "No, Louis, you can't run from me. I've come for you." The haze thickened. This wasn't working. Instead of coaxing him back, she was frightening him. His guilt hung heavy in the air. "That's it, isn't it?" she asked. "You don't think you deserve to come back. You think I'm angry with you?" The fog swirling around Zéolie was consuming her. She changed her tactic.

"Louis," she whispered. "Please, come back to me. I'm not angry with you." Zéolie stopped to listen. How would she know if he heard her? "I know you did what I asked you to do. It was the only way to stop her. You knew that then." The fog thinned some as she spoke. Light began to filter through. "Listen to me, Louis. You can't keep going like this. Please, Louis, please come back to me. I—I love you, Louis. Do you hear me?" she called into the haze. "*I love you!*"

Fog shifted, warming and lightening. In front of her, through the depths of the haze, a shadow slowly stepped forward. Her thoughts drifted back for an instant to her time in the haze between life and death when Camille materialized from the mist. The shadow in front of her didn't form from the mist like her grandmother had, rather, he stepped through it.

Zéolie's heart raced as Louis stood at the edge of his own oblivion. "Louis!" she cried.

His eyes were heavy and sad. "Zéolie, you shouldn't have come here."

"You're going to have to do a lot more than kill me to get rid of me, Louis Saucier," she said, standing her ground.

"I don't deserve you," he said, dropping his eyes.

She took a step towards him, testing his resolve. She could read his thoughts, wracked with guilt for murdering the woman he loved more than life itself. If Zéolie was going to convince him to come back, she was going to have to get him past that. One more step closer. He flinched but didn't move. Another step. "Louis, I need you to look at me."

He raised his eyes but not his head.

"Good," she said smiling. "What do you see?"

"My heart."

"And you're mine." Two more steps. He watched her intently but didn't move. "My heart, Louis. You're my heart. I can't live without you."

"You're wrong," he said, his voice breaking. "You can't live *because* of me."

One more step and she could touch him. "This isn't you, Louis. You're stronger than this. I *need you* to be stronger than this."

Louis shook his head, curls falling onto his forehead. You don't need me. Look at you. Strong, beautiful, powerful." His eyes took her in for the first time. "You never needed me."

Zéolie took his hand in hers. It was neither warm nor cold. Like a mirage. "I love you, and I need you more than you know." She put her hands on either side of his face. "Look at me, Louis. Really look." Words began to swirl around her. They were calling her back. *No*, she thought, *not yet. I'm so close!*

Louis could hear them, too. His eyes left hers as he searched for where the words were coming from. "Do you hear them?" he asked.

"Yes, I hear them," she said.

"I hear them all the time, but I don't understand what they mean."

Zéolie put a slender finger under his chin and turned his face back to hers. "Come with me and I'll show you. Come with me, my love." Easing herself up onto her toes, her lips found his.

Stiff and resistant at first, he slowly softened into her embrace and slid his arm around her waist, pulling her close. As he held her, the fog began to dissipate, taking his guilt with it. The last time he held her, she was cold and lifeless. The woman in his arms now was warm and genuinely alive.

"I'm sorry, Zéolie. I'm so sorry," he said. Fingers brushed through her long black hair.

Zéolie shook her head. "No, Louis. I'm sorry. I didn't think about what it would do to you. That you would have to live with what I asked you to do."

Louis let her go and stepped back as words continued to swirl around them. "There wasn't time to think." He paced for a minute as she watched his face. Thoughts she tried not to eavesdrop on did battle in his mind. Guilt struggled with justification. Love struggled with self-loathing. Words swelled in intensity, threatening to pull her out of his mind before he had a chance to make it up.

She had to do something. There was an eternity for him to struggle with his own doubt, but she didn't have an eternity anymore. "Louis, I need you to come back with me. I need your help." Her voice sharpened as she sensed time running out.

"What's happened?" Louis asked, sensing the urgency in her voice.

Zéolie started talking fast and frantic, trying to explain as much as she could before the words pulled her out of his mind. "I wish I knew. When she sent me back, Camille said I wasn't finished. I've tried to get her to talk to me, but she won't. Just signals I can't understand. Then, when Julien started talking about his dead uncle, she almost knocked me down."

"Julien? Y—your father?"

Words tumbled out of her mouth, tripping over each other in their haste for being heard. "No, he's a young man in town from Paris. Julien Haydel. He came to my house looking for his mother but hasn't been able to find her. I can't help but think Julien has something to do with what she brought me back for. Then, he started talking about an uncle and Camille—"

The police officer in Louis interrupted. "Wait, why would he come to your house looking for his mother?"

"It was the address on her letter. No one in town's heard of the woman. Something about all this isn't right. I'm telling you, Louis, there's more to this, and Camille's trying to get my attention." She grabbed his hands. The words were getting more fervent. "Louis, *please*. I love you, and I need your help. Please come back to me!"

With a nod of his head, she was thrown back into the stone room under the convent. His eyes fluttered then eased open. Louis looked up at the three relieved women standing over him. The voodoo priestess, Zéolie, and the mother superior. His brows knit in confusion.

"It's alright, Louis," Mother Micheaux said. "We'll explain it all when you're stronger. Welcome back."

FOURTEEN

Nighttime in New Orleans settled in sultry and warm despite the occasional puff of air from the riverfront. Boats slid silently past the candlelit city or bade a deep farewell with the throatiness of a ship's horn. Stars peered through the damp and haze at the people threading through tight streets and tighter banquettes. Some hurried home to families, some to questionable occupations, and others to entertainment.

Julien fought with a contrary necktie for twenty minutes of what seemed like forever as the words he wanted to say to Zéolie played on a constant loop in his mind.. Fingers that deftly tied the damn thing any other day were useless lumps of flesh fumbling at the silk. Frustration got the best of him and he flung the tie on the dressing table. As it landed, the glass lamp globe next to the tie shattered and the flame leaped and sizzled before settling back down. Shielding his face from the glass and heat, Julien instinctively held up his hand. Shards suspended inches from his palm and the heat couldn't touch him. His mouth gaped wide as a surge of something strange tingled through him, like standing too close to a lightning strike. Screwing up the courage to move, he pushed his hand away from him. The splintered glass followed. He moved it to the side, and the glass moved, too. Easing towards the ground, he pulled the glittering pieces to the wood planked floor and released them. Crouched over the glass, he heard a woman's voice like an echo through his mind, laughing low and deep. A sound he'd heard before only in dreams.

A cold chill settled over him as he stared at the hands he had cursed only moments before for not being able to tie a simple necktie. Now, they seemed foreign and strange. The words he wanted so badly to be perfect for Zéolie vanished from his mind, lost to swirling thoughts of floating glass and a haunting laugh. "I don't understand," he whispered as his eyes shifted their gaze from his fingers to the shards on the floor. "This is impossible." The low laugh in the depths of his mind seemed amused by his disbelief. Julien shook his head trying to force himself back into sane thoughts again, but the strange emotional cocktail of power and confusion held on tight. It wasn't until the tiny brass clock on the dressing table chimed that Julien was brought back to the present reality of being late to his own party.

Dressed in the finest of Monsieur Gaspard's cloth confections, Julien made his way to Royal Street and the home of the Marchons as thoughts tumbled wildly through his head. Words he wanted to say to Zéolie tripped over the laugh that mocked him from his dreams. Images of holding shards of glass suspended in front of him warred with his ideas of what was realistically possible. The tingling of electricity ebbed but didn't go away. Instead, it seemed to settle in his trembling hands, pricking his palms.

As much as Julien wanted to tell Zéolie what had happened, he knew what he would sound like. A raving lunatic. Already on the hunt for a mother who didn't exist, he couldn't risk coming off more insane than he already did. No, she couldn't know about the glass. Gaining distance from his bedroom, the possibility of it even happening began to fade. What if he had imagined the whole thing? What if he was losing his mind or had contracted some strange tropical disease that made its victim delusional? Until he knew for certain what he had seen, there was no way he was mentioning it to the women waiting to celebrate his twenty-first birthday.

Slowing his pace on the last block, he struggled to focus his thoughts. *Don't be a fool*, Julien thought. *Smile. Laugh. Enjoy the party, but for God's sake, watch what you say.* Sizzling fingertips reached for the brass knocker, tingling harder, but not jolting, as skin met brass. With a deep breath to steel nerves threatening to betray him, Julien let the heavy carved metal drop.

A man peered at him through a crack in the door, then opened it. White teeth split the brown face in a wide grin as Madame Marchon's servant greeted him. "Michie Haydel! Happy birthday to ya."

Julien smiled back. "Thank you, Isaiah." Handing his hat to Isaiah, Julien followed him through the house to the courtyard. Zéolie's was a lush jungle of herbs and flowers, but the Marchons' was spacious and welcoming. Near the tiered fountain in the center, a table and chairs had been set up for dinner. Gathered around the fountain with champagne flutes in hand were the Marchons, Zéolie, Mother Micheaux, and a handful of the closer acquaintances from town.

Madame Fontaine, the small rotund woman who owned the boarding house he lived in, bounced over to greet him. "Oh, Monsieur Haydel! Happy birthday! Isn't it a beautiful party?" Her chubby hands waved at the table, flowers, glittering china, and silverware.

Julien grinned over her shoulder at Zéolie who was doing her best not to giggle at the sweetly enthusiastic woman. "It is, Madame, and I'm happy you could join us for the occasion." He bent over her hand, kissing it lightly. She blushed, giggled, and went to get another glass of champagne.

"Am I late?" Julien asked Zéolie. "It seems she's had a good start on the champagne already."

Zéolie chuckled and sipped her own glass. "I think she may have come that way. She got here about ten minutes ago."

"That explains why she's always smiling. She's smashed." Julien laughed and took the glass Isaiah handed him.

"Smashed sounds like a good way to go through life," Celeste said with her hand outstretched. She smiled warmly at Julien and added, "Although, the perpetual hangover that comes with it is less inviting."

Julien kissed her hand as Listette said, "You'd know." Celeste shot a seething look at her sister, who had gained miraculous confidence on her own turf. "Well, you would," Lisette said and walked off with a toss of her head.

Celeste's anger at her sister shifted to embarrassment as she turned back to Julien. "If you'll excuse me," she said quietly, then went to talk to the happily inebriated Madame Fontaine who was discussing the latest fashion in women's hats with Monsieur Gaspard.

"What was that about?" Julien asked.

Zéolie opened her mouth to answer but thought better of it and shrugged. She wasn't about to get into the horrors of her mother's funeral antics in the middle of his birthday party. "There's no telling with Celeste."

"I see you managed to talk her out of the acrobats," Julien said.

"Only just. You can thank Madame Marchon for that one. It was only when she told Celeste she'd have to pay them with her own money that she finally gave up on the idea."

Julien laughed. "Then thank God for Celeste's extravagant shopping habits and a modest allowance."

Zéolie raised her champagne flute. "I'll drink to that." She and Julien drained their glasses.

"Can I get you some more?" Julien asked. "It's a party, after all."

With a nod, Zéolie gave him her glass. As he took it, his hand brushed hers and a sting of electricity raced up her arm. Her hand jerked back, just stopping it from hitting the bricks of the courtyard.

"Are you alright?" he asked.

"I'm fine," she insisted. "Sorry about that." Certain it was another signal from Camille, Zéolie couldn't tell him what caused her to react like that.

"That was close," Julien said. *And I've had enough broken glass for one night.* "Maybe we should sit down."

A short, forced laugh. "Maybe so," Zéolie said as Julien led her to the edge of the fountain that seemed to rise up from the red brick of the courtyard floor. She pretended to be settling her skirt around her as Julien went to the side table where the champagne was being iced. Thoughts raced with her pulse as she tried to decipher what Camille reacted to. Nothing was said about his family or anything else for that matter. Just pedantic small talk. Why would she be trying to get Zéolie's attention now?

There was no time to figure out what sparked Camille's reaction before Julien returned with her drink. He sat beside her with a slight smile, but there was something on his mind. Nervous fingers tapped on his glass. She knew that tapping. She'd seen him do the same thing with a tarot card on her balcony before he left abruptly. "Something wrong?" she asked gently.

"N—no," he said with a start. He had been deep into his own thoughts, trying to remember what he'd carefully planned to say to her before the lamp shattered and he caught the shards. The words were gone, adrift in a sea of broken glass.

A ringing of silver on crystal stopped any more questions from Zéolie as Madame Marchon got their attention to call them to the table. "If you'll find your places, we'll begin dinner."

Madame Marchon had enough forethought to put Julien at the head of the table with herself and Zéolie on either side, keeping Celeste's rampant flirting from his immediate vicinity. Madame Fontaine and Monsieur Gaspard next to them. Then, an older man, a Monsieur Peyaud, who was a boarder at Madame Fontaine's as well, and the Marchon girls on the far end. True to her tradition, Madame Marchon left the seat at the foot of the table vacant, but dishes set, for the memory of her husband.

As each course was brought and wine poured, Julien began to

relax and talk easily with the women on either side of him. Madame Marchon kept the conversation to polite subjects of news, weather, and the like. Monsieur Gaspard was eager to know how the new wardrobe he'd fashioned was suiting the honored guest, and Madame Fontaine was happy to supply the fact that she's noticed more than a few young women's heads turn as he passed her boarding house. Julien blushed and Celeste winked, which made Julien blush more. Another glass of wine and he was flirting back.

Zéolie watched Julien leaning closer to Celeste instead of making polite moves away from her advances. Her heart belonged to Louis, but Julien didn't know that. Maybe she was wrong about how he felt about her. Maybe it really was Celeste that kept him lingering around her house. Even Madame Marchon raised an eyebrow at Julien and Celeste lingering a few more minutes than she liked in the darker corner of the courtyard after dinner. It wasn't one of disapproval as much as surprise.

In the shadows, Julien walked with Celeste's arm threaded through the crook of his. There was no flirtation, no inuendo in Celeste's words this time. There was something genuine about her smile that surprised him. "This isn't right," he said, stopping and pulling her arm out of his.

Celeste's dark eyes looked up at him confused. "I'm sorry?"

"I—I mean," he stammered, "I'm afraid I might be giving you the wrong idea. You see—"

Celeste held up a hand. "You don't have to say it." Her smile only barely covered her disappointment as she tried to recover her coy playfulness. "I know." Her long fingers brushed the back of his hand. "Now, let me take you back to where you really want to be."

With a wink and a crook of her finger, she led him across the courtyard to the table where Zéolie chatted with Madame Fontaine. The round face of the equally round woman was flushed with inebriation.

"Zéolie," Celeste said, "I believe I've occupied the guest of honor long enough. Your turn." Tossing a grin over her shoulder at the two of them, she sashayed over to Lisette and Monsieur Gaspard, taking Madame Fontaine with her.

Julien shuffled his feet uncomfortably, suddenly without the confidence the alcohol gave him, and Zéolie enjoyed letting him dangle for a moment before she rescued him. Running a finger around the rim of her glass, she grinned up at Julien. "Another drink?" she asked.

He shook his dark head. "No, I think I've had more than I need."

"A walk, then?"

Julien's heart pounded in his ears as the words he wanted to say flooded back to him. Words that left with the shattering of glass and returned with the soft clink of her champagne flute on the table as she stood and held out her hand. Electricity tingled through him as he reached for her. A jolt of static went through them both as they touched. Eyes wide, both jumped back. "What the hell was that?" Julien asked.

"I—I don't know. You felt it, too?" Zéolie asked.

Julien nodded. "Must be something in the air," he said, knowing it was a weak deflection.

"Maybe," Zéolie answered, knowing it was nothing of the kind. In the back of her mind, a faint echo of her mother's laugh sent a chill through her. Wrapping her arms around her waist, she forced a smile and walked away.

Julien followed, unsure of what was happening but knowing this was his chance to say the words that were threatening to tumble out of his mouth. The moon over the courtyard was lost in the torchlight. A sliver of a crescent peeking through clouds that slid across the sky. Julien looked up at it, silently pleading with it to shed light on whatever was happening to him.

Zéolie leaned against the brick wall and looked up at the moon, silently pleading with it to shed light on whatever Camille was trying to tell her. "Pretty, isn't it?" she asked.

"Beautiful," Julien answered, not looking at the moon anymore. Zéolie blushed, which only made her more stunning. The pounding of his heart in his ears began to do battle with the woman's low laugh in his mind that got stronger the closer he was to telling Zéolie how he felt. If he was completely honest with himself, the laugh had changed from amused to mocking, though he had no idea how or why.

He struggled against light-headedness and the chorus of sounds to find what he wanted to say. Pushing the laugh to the back of his mind, he focused on the words. "Zéolie, since I came to the city, you've been so kind, so welcoming. I—I don't know if I would've stayed this long if it hadn't been for you." He wanted so badly to reach out and touch her face, but feared shocking her again, so he let his hand drop as he paced instead. "All this searching for my mother has led me to one dead end after another. I may not have found what I came here looking for," deep breath, "but I've found something else. Something more."

He paused, searching her face for anything that would give him hope. Nothing. Just her usual focused attention on his words. Courage faltering, he picked up his pace. If he was going to say what was on his mind, he needed to just get it out.

Energy hummed in Zéolie's veins as Julien talked. Any doubts she had when he was walking with Celeste were wrong. She knew what he was trying to say, and she could have easily cut him off, but part of her wanted to hear him say it. She didn't know why. Her heart belonged to Louis, but something in her wanted to hear Julien say exactly how he felt about her.

"Zéolie," Julien began, resisting taking her hands in his, "your kindness, your attention, have made New Orleans seem more like home than Paris ever did. Growing up there, I never wanted for anything, but there was no warmth. In a city known for love, I was alone. Then, I came here and found the warmth I was missing. Not—not the weather, I mean, real warmth. Friendship. And—" He took a breath and stood as close to her as he dared. "More than that," he whispered. "Zéolie, I didn't plan on falling in love with you, but I have, with all my heart."

The night hung thick between them. Shadows of palm leaves moved languidly as Julien held his breath waiting on her to say something. Anything. Electricity surged through him. Each second she was silent, the surge became harder to contain. His stomach clenched and sweat beaded on his forehead. *Why doesn't she answer?* he thought.

Zéolie's mind spun. He'd said it. She got what she wanted, but now he was waiting on a response. She only had one answer for the boy who poured his soul at her feet. It lay there in anguish waiting on her to hold it in her arms, but she couldn't. Now, standing in the silence, she grasped for words that would soften the blow. "Julien," she said at last.

His heart thrummed as she spoke.

"Welcoming you into my home and into our lives has brought so much enjoyment, not just to me, but to all of us." Trying to take his intent gaze from her face, she held her hand out to the group gathered around the fountain. It didn't work. *God, I have to do this.* Zéolie pressed the palms of her hands flat against the brick wall behind her to steady herself. "Julien, I'm flattered that you count me as a friend, but you need to understand that's all I'll ever be. I don't—I can't love you. It's just—just complicated." Fingernails dug into the mortar between the bricks. His face contorted and the echo of laughter grew louder in her ears.

Pain shot through Julien's chest, radiating from his heart. Heartbreak collided with anger as words sputtered. "But—but the night we sat in the dark, the flirting over the balcony rail. It meant *nothing* to you? *Nothing?!*" Heat settled in his hands, pulsing and sizzling uncontrollably. The low laugh cackled and shrieked. His mind spun wildly as images from dreams flooded him. The swamp, the laughter, chaos and fire. *What's happening to me?* He panicked and put his hands over his ears to shut out the noise, but it was coming from inside. Nothing helped. It grew louder and more manic. Something deep inside of Julien began to crumble as his heart withered at

Zéolie's feet and a whirlwind of raging electricity tore through him. Hands pulsing. Head pounding. Heart breaking.

Zéolie's eyes widened in shock as Julien turned on his heel and strode across the courtyard away from her. Unable to contain the energy anymore, he released it as he passed the table. Glasses exploded where they stood, china splintered, and silverware stood straight up on their handles twisting wildly. Without another word, Julien Haydel strode out of the courtyard into the night, leaving his birthday guests in stunned silence.

CHAPTER

FIFTEEN

oubt evaporated as Julien vanished into the night. No more lingering questions about whether he was connected to whatever Camille was warning them about. No. Now the only question was how.

How had he obliterated an entire dining table of glassware and china with a flick of his fingers? How did he hide the power all the time he was with them? How did Zéolie and Mother Micheaux not see it coming? How could they stop him if he turned on them?

Leaving Madame Marchon and her indomitable tact to clean up the mess and the questions of the remaining guests, Zéolie swung into the back of the carriage, not waiting on Lucien to help her inside. There was one place answers could be found, and she tore through the night toward it.

The clattering of hooves and wheels triggered lamplight to appear in the front windows as the nuns stirred to see what was happening outside. Lucien jumped down and nodded to Zéolie, who stayed put. A few words to the servant at the door then he was back in the driver's seat. Crunching gravel as they pulled around the rear of the convent gave way to the soft silence of grass. Time stretched wearily as they waited in the dark. Zéolie's heart pounded and the laugh she thought she'd broken free of when she died settled once more into her mind. Hollow, fragmented, but definitely there.

A spider's thread of golden light shot through the crack in the door and Zéolie was out of the carriage, chasing the light into the darkness of the convent.

Silently, she followed the mother superior through the familiar near-darkness of the passage into the stone room below. Another sliver of light after the grinding of metal on metal as the door eased open. Mama Nell was on her feet, guarded against the unexpected intrusion. "What da hell is goin' on, Zéolie? You look like you seen a ghost!"

"Something like that," she answered.

"Sit, sit," the priestess said clearing bundles of drying herbs off a chair for her. What had once been a stark, underused room had become more like the cozy and mysterious cabin in the swamp. Zéolie sat down and spread her hands out on her knees. Sweating palms left marks on the linen of her dress.

Mother Micheaux crouched in front of her. "*Chérie*, tell us what happened."

Zéolie recounted the events of the evening in detail, unsure of what might spark some glimmer of understanding in either of them. Everything from the meal to the glittering explosion of Julien's exit.

The nun and priestess exchanged glances but focused their attention on Zéolie as she talked. It wasn't until she was finished that Mother Micheaux said, "I think I know what's going on here, but I don't want to be right."

Mama Nell nodded as though an age-old mystery had been revealed.

"Will someone please let me in on it?" Zéolie begged.

Mama Nell shook her head. "It's not for us to be tellin' you, child." She shook her head, her tignon a deep crimson in the lamp-light. "That's for Camille to do."

"God damnit!" Zéolie cursed. "She doesn't *tell* me anything! If she wanted to tell me, she could have done it by now. It's not like we haven't given her plenty of chances."

Mother Micheaux stood in calm contrast to Zéolie's frustration and smoothed her robes. "I think she needs one more chance. And, this time, we'll get it right."

"What about Louis?" Zéolie asked. In the corner, Louis slept soundly, but not with the same troubled sleep as before. It was deep and peaceful.

Mama Nell glanced over at him. "I'll wake him. We'll need him to ground us, so to speak. If somethin' happens, he'll be on the outside to get help."

Zéolie wanted to be the one to wake Louis. To touch his forehead and push the curls out of his face. To kiss him. But there was no time for tenderness, and she was certain he'd been drugged to sleep that soundly. It would take another mixture from the priestess to rouse him.

"What do you need me to do?" Mother Micheaux asked Nell.

The priestess never looked up from her work at the table where she was taking drops from various vials and combining them in a shot glass. "Go get Squire."

The nun hesitated. "Are you sure? If he says anything—"

Mama Nell laughed a ripple of music through the room. "And what would he say? He knows I've been down here all this time. If he was goin' to say somethin', he'd a done it by now. An' if he did, well, I'd join the order tomorrow!" Mama Nell said with a grin at Zéolie as Mother Micheaux slipped noiselessly out the door. "Some nun I'd be!"

With a shake of her head, she said, "The boy can't talk. He's mute. Can't hear neither. But he can feel a beat, and that's what we need 'im for now. Can't dance up some spirits without a drummer!" She held up the shot glass and examined the murky substance in the lamplight. It slid around the inside of the glass as she swirled it to mix it. A few more drops from one of the small brown vials and she was satisfied.

Zéolie tried to think of a way to ask the obvious question without stirring up sadness in Mama Nell. "Is Squire your—I mean, did you and—Never mind. It's not my business."

Mama Nell winked at her. "Is Squire my son?" Zéolie nodded. "No, *chérie*. Never had a child of my own. Took in a few over the years. Life deals folks some pretty bad hands now and then. It's not the children's fault. But, no, Squire's not mine. In fact, you've probably met 'im."

"Where?"

"Here. With the secrets we've been guardin' all this time, Mother and I couldn't trust just anyone to run messages for us. For a long time, it was Squire's mama, Eliza."

Zéolie's brow knit. "How did you know you could trust her?"

A grin flickered across the priestess' face as she sprinkled herbs into the shot glass. "Squire's afflictions are somethin' passed down from his mama." A mossy green eye winked. "Even if she could read 'em, she'd've had the devil of a time gettin' anyone to understan' 'er, much less believe 'er. An' she was well paid for her silence. When she died, Squire took over. Truth be told, he took over a while before that. His mama was in bad shape for a long time, but Mother Micheaux couldn't turn 'er out. The sisters took care of 'er, an' I did what I could where they couldn't."

"That was kind of you," Zéolie said.

"Understan' this: you take care of your own. Those that's been good to you, and loyal. Always. When they go on, they return the favor."

"Go on?"

"When they die, *chérie*."

Or they torment you instead, she thought as her mother's laugh rumbled in the back of her mind.

Hinges ached as the door eased open. "Go on, child," Mother Micheaux said. "It's alright."

From the darkness of the stairwell, a boy of about twelve with velvety ebony skin stepped nervously through the door with Mother

Micheaux's hand putting enough pressure on his shoulders to steer him where she wanted him.

"Why does she talk to him?" Zéolie whispered. "He can't hear her."

"Well, that time he couldn't 'cause she was behin' 'im. Most times he can read her lips. He don' know what the actual words are she's sayin', but he's made up the meanin' of 'em pretty good. He's usually pretty close on what someone wants of 'im."

She waved the nervous boy over to the seat Zéolie had been sitting in earlier. The only uncluttered surface in the room. Squire sat obediently, darting dark eyes at Zéolie. Trying to ease his nerves, Zéolie smiled at him. After a moment, he attempted a smile back at her. It became clear that he wasn't sure why he was brought into the room under the convent, and she didn't know how to tell him he wasn't in trouble. "I don't think he knows why he's here," Zéolie said. "He looks worried."

"You didn' tell 'im?" Mama Nell asked the nun.

"Tell him what? You didn't tell me why you wanted him."

Mama Nell chuckled to herself. "Lord, you're right." She glided to the far corner of the room where odds and ends had been shoved out of the way and returned with a small drum. It stood about two feet high, was narrower in the middle of the base, with beaded cording in a diamond pattern around the body of the drum. The head was tightly pulled animal skin. Mama Nell set it on the floor at his feet and his face softened into understanding. The priestess held up her hand to him as a signal to wait until she was ready. His hands flattened over the skin of the drum, getting a feel for it before they settled onto the edges waiting for the signal to start.

"First things first," Nell said, picking up the shot glass and carrying it over to where Louis slept. "He's not goin' to like this any, but he's gotta get it down. Zéolie, I could sure use your help, *chérie*." Zéolie nodded and followed her aunt. Mama Nell knelt by the cot and gently lifted his head. "Hold his arms. It's nasty stuff an' he's gonna try to knock it away."

"I'm ready," Zéolie said, holding Louis' wrists down on the cot.

"Once I get 'im to swallow it, you can let 'im go." In one fluid movement, Mama Nell lifted his chin, parted his mouth, and shot the liquid to the back of his throat. Louis gagged and sputtered, choking on the foul concoction. Instinctively his hands jerked upwards, but Zéolie leaned her weight onto his wrists until Mama Nell let go of his jaw. "Let 'im go. He's got it down."

As she released him, Louis' hands flew to his mouth, his eyes wide. "What the hell was that?" he demanded.

"The only way we were wakin' you up in time," the priestess said simply.

"Ugh," he groaned. "That was awful." His eyes settled on Zéolie standing at his feet twisting her fingers. "But worth it. Zéolie! What are you doing here?"

She smiled down at him. "I came to check on you." Zéolie knelt down and gently kissed the corner of his mouth.

"You're a terrible liar. Always have been." He hid his apprehension behind a grin. "As much as I'd love to believe that, something's happened, hasn't it?"

"Yes." Zéolie answered, the smile running away from her face.

Whatever the priestess gave Louis evaporated the haze of sleep from his mind, but his body was a little slower coming to. He struggled for a moment to push himself up to sitting against the wall. Mother Micheaux helped get a pillow behind his back, then sat on the edge of the bed. "I wish we had time for a detailed story, but you'll have to settle for an abbreviated version. Julien Haydel had his sights set on Zéolie, but when she turned him down, he showed her, and everyone at the Marchon's, what he's capable of."

"He had his sights set on *you*?" Louis asked Zéolie.

"*Chérie*," Mother Micheaux said, "you've missed the point entirely."

Mama Nell laughed. "Not entirely, but he was a little wide of the mark."

Louis blushed. "Sorry. What was it he's capable of?"

"Shattering an entire dinner table setting with a wave of his hand," Zéolie said. "Complete with spinning flatware."

Louis tried to mask his concern. "At least he's got flair."

Mama Nell stood and smoothed her skirt, straightening the scarves draping her waist. "Damn sight more'n that. He's got power an' a broken heart. Dangerous combination."

"It was strange to watch," Zéolie said. "Julien was always unsure of himself, kind, and funny once he warmed up to someone. But what I saw tonight—I don't understand it. It was as if—as if there was something more than heartbreak in him. Something darker. His face—it changed, hardened. He scared me before he ever took his anger out on the table."

Mother Micheaux looked up at Zéolie from the edge of the bed. "There's more to this, I'm afraid. If I'm right, he's more dangerous than we think."

Zéolie asked, "What do you mean?"

The nun shook her head. "We'll let Camille explain that one."

Louis was confused. "I thought she wasn't talking."

A shadow settled over Mother Micheaux's features. "We'll see about that."

Part of Zéolie went cold as the laugh echoed again. A shadow of her past that she couldn't shake. At least, she hoped a shadow was all it was. "How do we start?" she asked.

"Carefully," Mama Nell said. She went over to the table and began moving things around as she talked. Putting vials away, clearing dried herbs, and setting out candles. "Up 'til now, you've tried simply connectin' in the only way you know to call her. It's not enough or she'd come through the veil. For some reason, she can't. Either it's us, or it's her. One side or the other's got somethin' stoppin' 'em."

"Like what?" Louis asked.

Mama Nell shrugged her graceful shoulders. "Could be anythin'. Fear, someone else in the way, guilt. Who knows?"

"But," Louis pushed, "if we don't know what's in the way, how do we get it *out* of the way?"

"Leave that to me," the priestess said, picking up a cigar, biting off the end, and spitting it onto the floor. Laying it across a shot glass on the table, she set to work on the floor. "We take turns," she said, handing Mother Micheaux a broom. It was more like a bundle of sticks with frayed ends tied with brightly colored cord. "From the back corner towards the door."

With measured intention, the nun began to sweep the floor as Mama Nell reminded Zéolie of the practice of pushing negative energy out the door to make room for positive energy. Each one cleared the space as Louis watched from the cot. Mama Nell went last. By the time it was her turn, she'd lit candles on the table, set out a bottle of rum, and lit a small chunk of charcoal that popped and hissed in a small cast iron pot.

"Louis," Mama Nell said, "it's time. We'll need you on your feet, ready in case somethin' happens, but on the outside of the circle. If anythin' goes wrong, get help."

Louis face darkened. "What could go wrong? What am I looking for?"

The priestess shook her head. "Hard to say, but you'll know when ya see it."

"Lucien's waiting outside. Go out the back corridor. You'll find him," Zéolie said.

Louis nodded and stood beside the cot, but outside the circle Mother Micheaux was making on the floor with salt. Words flowed from her mouth, silent and intent as she worked stooped over, rhythmically dipping her fingertips into the salt well and sprinkling it on the floor. Once the ring was complete, she gave the salt to Mama Nell.

The priestess poured a handful of salt into another bowl and added a pink, chalky substance to it. Nodding at Squire to begin, she knelt in the center of the ring in the middle of the floor. In time with the slow rhythm the boy played on the drum like he'd done for her so many times before, Mama Nell's fingers dipped into the substance and began making shapes on the floor. With deft movements of her fingertips and twisting of her wrist, a delicate and intricate shape began to emerge as pinched salt was released on the ground. Perfect circles, straight lines, swirls, and crosses merged into one singular form, growing in symmetry. As she worked, she sang. The song blended words Zéolie now knew from the nun with old words from a different place. Raw and fierce, loving and bold. Mama Nell's voice filled the chamber and resonated off the stone walls in sweet rich tones. Notes dropped onto the salt image in front of her and floated back up again, pulling magic from the air.

The intricate symbol finished, Mama Nell stood and held the bowl high above her head, calling down the spirits to bless her work, asking their approval of her design—a delicate welcome mat for the ones whose help she sought. Backing away from the image on the floor, she set the bowl down on the table.

Squire picked up the pace on the drum. The priestess bent her knees slightly and turned one foot out, barely lifting her toes off the ground before setting them down again. Ankle turned back inward, weight shifted slightly, other foot turned out, toes up, ankle in, repeat. Right, left, right, left. In steady movements, the dance began.

Slow and deliberate at first, then becoming bigger and more fluid. She held her swirling skirt away from her legs to give them room to move. Her head swayed side to side as the rhythm soaked into her body and took over. Mama Nell turned slowly, her feet keeping up a steady rocking from her heels to the balls of her feet and back down again. Squire picked up the pace again and the dance sped up, gaining intensity with each movement.

Zéolie watched as Nell began to circle her, pulling her toward the symbol in the center. Mother Micheaux held her hands clasped together at her chest in wordless prayer just inside the circle of salt. Nell's dance became frenzied. Energy built in Zéolie's body, tingling and surging. Whatever this ritual was, it was working.

Squire's beat shifted again to something slower, less predictable, but still rhythmic as Nell's dance eased back down to slow, exaggerated movements until it finally ceased. The priestess stood still, spent and flushed, with her feet on the edge of the symbol. More words. Something about opening gates and meeting Papa Legba in a crossroad, then words Zéolie didn't know.

Mother Micheaux walked slowly to the center of the circle, being careful not to let her long skirt touch the salt drawing, and stood beside Zéolie. "She's called on every power she knows, so now we make them feel welcome here," the nun explained. "First, the food," she said as Mama Nell raised the silver blade high. She sliced into a piece of fruit, took a bite, then handed pieces to Zéolie and Mother Micheaux. "We eat with the spirits, then leave the rest for them." The priestess placed the fruit on a small plate on the table next to a flickering candle stump.

"Now, the drink," Mother Micheaux said.

"It's like Communion," Zéolie whispered. The nun nodded.

Mama Nell used her teeth to pull the cork from the bottle and the smell of rum wafted over them. She poured a generous amount into a cup and handed it first to Mother Micheaux. The mother superior drank, then handed it to Zéolie who did the same. The rich dark rum burned going down and warmed her insides. Zéolie gave the cup back to the priestess, who took a sip, swallowed, then took another. Throwing her head back, Mama Nell spit rum between her teeth showering the altar. Candles popped and leaped in the fuel sprayed on them. Bottles, herbs, coins and trinkets on the altar glittered in their new raiment of rum. Gingerly, she set the small glass on the center of the table in front of the scattering of offerings.

"You're the channel, *chérie*," Mama Nell said. "So, we do some special cleansin' of your energy." She dipped her fingers into the rum and sprinkled Zéolie from head to toe, murmuring as drops were thrown from graceful fingertips. Rubbing her hands together to dry them, the priestess picked up the cigar she'd left on the shot glass. Holding it up to the candlelight, she carefully examined it for flaws before rolling it between her palms, smoothing the outside of it.

Licking her lips, she placed it between her teeth. Then, she leaned into the largest candle on the table. Cheeks hollowed as she sucked in the candle flame that played tug of war with the end of the cigar.

Thick gray smoke poured from Nell's mouth as she made sure the whole end was lit. After a few puffs to make sure it wasn't going to go out, she turned and faced her niece. Zéolie was struck at the image in front of her. Tall, liquid grace wrapped in scarves and glittering bracelets, soft mossy eyes and burgundy lips under a deep orange tignon. A picture of exotic femininity made gritty and raw by the cigar clenched tightly between white teeth.

Mama Nell's slender hands lifted Zéolie's arms out to either side. Gently pushing air out from her mouth through the cigar, smoke billowed from the glowing end as the priestess bathed Zéolie in it. Thick smoke curled around Zéolie's arms, stung her eyes, and ran tendrils through her dark hair as the priestess worked. Slowly, deliberately, she cleansed every inch of Zéolie's figure before she was satisfied and took the cigar out of her mouth. Turning back to the table, she added the stump of smoldering tobacco to the spirit altar. Dropping a sliver of wood incense on the charcoal lump, Mama Nell turned back to the center as a sweet-smelling smoke rose up behind her adding to the haze hanging heavily in the air. Taking Zéolie's hands in hers, she said, "It's time."

The three women took their places around the salt image in the middle. Each planted her feet wide for stability and took the hands of the women on either side. Louis, who had been rapt in the ceremony, snapped to attention as the seance began. He had no idea what to do if anything went wrong. What could he do against forces that might break through their magic? Forces he himself had seen and felt without being able to stop them. He stood guard but knew full well he was useless.

Electricity hummed through the hands of the three women in the circle. The dark nun, the graceful priestess, and the resurrected witch. It pulsed harder through their hands in rhythm, like a hoop with one strong point that circled through their bodies, as though it was a spinning ring in the center of them. For reasons she didn't understand, Zéolie could picture it. A thick black wheel laying on its side with a glowing green spot that surged by her on its way to her aunt and the mother superior, whirling faster as the pulse strengthened. The power in each of them hurled the energy onward to the next as the intensity gathered. Soon the pulse steadied to a regular pace as the connection settled.

"Use what we give you to reach Camille. Pull what you need from us. We'll stop you if it's more than we can spare," Mother Micheaux instructed.

Zéolie's dark eyes closed and, for a second, she thought her feet left the ground before she found her center. Focusing on the thrum of energy, she pushed distractions, including the relentless echo of her mother's laugh, to the back of her mind.

Blackness enveloped her. Thick and unyielding. Zéolie tried to push back against it, to find light somewhere, but she wasn't strong enough on her own. Imagining her chest opening to create a space for more than she had, she pulled energy from the nun and priestess. Thin glittering threads of white light streamed into the chasm. As she drew on the strength from the others, the darkness ebbed, and light began to push through until she was standing in a flood of shimmering white.

"Camille?" she called into the space around her. Her voice echoed in the vast emptiness. "Can you hear me?"

Nothing.

"I know you've been trying to tell me something. Nell's here, and Mother Micheaux. Please. We need you to tell us what's happening."

Mama Nell's voice from far away drifted into her mind. "Tell her who you're here to talk about."

Zéolie nodded but wasn't sure what the other two could see or hear. "Something happened tonight, Camille. I know you saw it. I need you to tell me what's happening to Julien Haydel." Energy surged and crackled around her at the mention of Julien's name.

"You know something, don't you? You're hiding something from me. Why?"

Silence. Pulsing energy in the empty space around her.

Zéolie sighed. This wasn't working. For weeks, Camille had been pricking her and almost knocking her over, but when given the chance to talk face-to-face, she hid. It didn't make sense. *Something in the way...guilt.* Mama Nell's words to Louis came back to her. "Camille, what's in the way? Is it something I've done?"

She waited. Silence.

"I wish I'd had the chance to know you, Camille," Zéolie said gently. "You know, I never got the chance to thank you." Somewhere in the vacuum, she knew her grandmother could hear her. "It couldn't have been easy to help me fight your own child. To try to destroy her. But you did."

More silence. More waiting.

"I can't imagine how it felt to watch your daughter become what she did. To turn from everything you'd taught her and wanted her to be. You gave up everything for Solène, and she became your deepest fear." Zéolie's voice was gentle. "I couldn't take her on by myself. The only reason we were able to stop her is because of you." She paused, tears welling up in her dark eyes, and blue veins pulling across pale cheeks. "Thank you," she choked on the words. "Thank you, Camille."

Humming energy intensified, full of emotion. Sadness and pain hovered around Zéolie like fog. A voice broke through the silence, soft and pained. "It was all my fault," it said.

"Camille?"

"All of this was *my* fault. *I knew.* I knew what she could become, and I did it anyway. My mother warned me. I didn't listen."

Guilt. "*Chérie*," Zéolie said, "this isn't' your fault. You *helped* me."

"No, it's all my fault. I loved him. He wanted children. I gave him Solène. I knew about his madness. I knew what could happen. It's my fault. It's *all* my fault."

The pain was crushing.

"You couldn't have known then. You only say that because of what you know now."

"No!" the voice cried. "I knew what he was. I saw it long before anyone else did. My poor love. My poor Jacques."

Shock ripped through Zéolie. She choked on the words. *"What did you say?"*

Camille was lost in her own sorrow, sobbing, "My poor Jacques. My poor, poor love. It's all my fault."

Pieces of the puzzle slammed into place for Zéolie. Camille knew Jacques was going mad but wanted to give the man she loved what he wanted. Knowing madness and magic could be disastrous, she got pregnant anyway, hoping Solène wouldn't inherit her father's insanity. Now, Camille blamed herself for everything that had happened to the family. All of the family, which seemed to include Julien. But the question now was how was Julien Haydel connected to Jacques, Camille, and Solène? Was the Jacques in Julien's story her grandfather? She needed to find out how everything was connected, but to do it, she'd have to get her grandmother out of her own personal hell.

"I know you blame yourself, but there's nothing you can do about that now. I *need you*. I need you to help me make this right."

Silence. Silence, not sobbing. She had her grandmother's attention.

"You owe the family this, Camille. You can't change the past, but you control what happens next. Make it count. Make it right." Zéolie held her breath. "Camille? Do you hear me?"

Silence. Then, "Mother Micheaux knows. She knows who Julien is."

Pain, anger, and sorrow mixed with the bitterness of fear deep inside her. These weren't Camille's emotions. They were coming from within, but they weren't hers, tangled in the energy she was drawing from the other two women. These emotions belonged to the mother superior. "No." The word was barely audible. "That's impossible."

Camille chuckled wryly. "You should know by now, Mother. Nothing is impossible." Darkness began to descend as the energy flow slowed. The mother superior had been rocked to her core and was struggling to keep the connection. Camille called into the gathering gloom, "I'm here, Zéolie, and I'll help you. You'll know what to do."

Mama Nell forced all the strength she could spare into Zéolie trying to pull her out of the trance safely before Mother Micheaux was drained completely. At the last instant, Zéolie's eyes flickered open, locking with the nun's before both of them dropped to the ground.

CHAPTER

SIXTEEN

"You're developin' a nasty habit of faintin' right when people need ya," Mama Nell told Zéolie, holding the girl's head in her lap on the ground.

"I'm sorry," Zéolie whispered. "I'll work on that." Consciousness was slow coming back to her after the seance, and the edges of the room were still fuzzy as she tried to sit up. Gentle pressure from Mama Nell's hand on her shoulder eased her back down for a few minutes more. "What happened? Mother Micheaux?"

"Shh, child," Mama Nell insisted. "She's fine. Louis' takin' care of 'er."

Zéolie eased her head over to look in the direction the priestess pointed and saw the aging nun in much the same position she was—on the floor where she had been standing, her head in Louis' lap. He had a damp cloth that he was folding to lay across her forehead. She didn't look as fine as her aunt said. "Did you hear her? Did you hear Camille?"

Mama Nell nodded and gently stroked Zéolie's dark hair. "We all did. Well, 'cept Louis, but I filled 'im in."

"Do you think she really knows something she hasn't told us?" Zéolie asked glancing at the mother superior.

Mama Nell sighed. "*Chérie*, that woman knows more secrets than we'll ever forget. I'm sure she knows things she hasn't told us, an' I'm sure she had damn good reasons for it." She eased Zéolie up to sitting. "An' she'll tell us when she's damn good an' ready. As for you, you look terrible. Time for tea. Louis, you, too."

Zéolie looked down at her hands since she couldn't see her own face. Blue veins streaked across pale white skin. "Fine."

By the time their tea was brewed, Mother Micheaux was awake and talking. "I know Camille said that I know, and it's possible I do, but there's someone I need to talk to first."

"And if you're right?" Zéolie asked. "If you *do* know what she's talking about?"

"Then, things are worse than we ever imagined. Find whatever words you can and pray Camille's wrong."

Dust thickly covered the books on shelves behind the heavy wooden desk in Mother Micheaux's convent office. Words that hadn't been read in years sat dormant under their fluffy blanket. One well-worn book was spared the neglectful housekeeping, although it hadn't been opened in a long time either. It was simply carried from place to place, a constant reminder of prayers that wouldn't come. Prayers that left her the day she broke her vow. Wrinkled fingers tapped the black book anxiously.

The mother superior paced, impatient for Squire to return with the response from the country. He'd left early that morning, and it was nearly sundown. Zéolie, Nell, and Louis had questions they wanted answers to and she was running out of ways to stall them. With Louis better and able to take care of himself more, Mother Micheaux sent Mama Nell back to the Quarter with Zéolie to check on the house and servants, keeping Louis at the convent. If she was right about Julien Haydel, Zéolie had no business being alone. She'd need Nell. Truthfully, she'd need them both, but that wasn't an option right now.

Footsteps in the hallway stopped her pacing as she braced for Squire's message. Seconds later, the boy's dark head peeked around the corner. Waving him quickly inside, she shut the door behind them. "Well? Did you see him?" Squire nodded. "What did he say?"

The boy held out a folded scrap of paper that had been bunched in his sweaty hand. The ink had smudged but was still legible.

I'll meet you, but not at the plantation house. There's a cabin on an inlet not far from there. Squire knows where it is. Noon tomorrow. ~JJH

"Fine. The cabin at noon," she grumbled to no one in particular since Squire couldn't read her lips as she paced. Realizing this, she turned and faced the boy. "Tomorrow morning. Early. We go," she said pointing at the note. He understood and gave a slight bow as he left.

RIDING SINCE DAWN, Mother Micheaux slowed her frantic pace, letting the horse breathe as she neared the cabin on the river. Squire rode ahead of her, keeping watch and guiding the way. True to his word, the meeting place was close to the plantation property, but far enough away that they wouldn't risk being seen.

Nestled against a horseshoe inlet of the Mississippi River, the wood planked cabin was usually used for a launch point for fishing boats. The shelter of the tree-lined curve kept the boats moored there safe from the high winds of storms or the raging of the current after heavy rains. Now, it would serve a very different purpose.

A black horse waited patiently tied to a post on the back side of the cabin. Squire hitched his horse, then helped Mother Micheaux off before securing hers. Prayers once again failed her as she steadied herself before knocking. Aged fingers curled as she rapped softly on the door. She wasn't sure why she was being so quiet. The person she was meeting knew she was there by the sounds of the horses, and it was no surprise visit.

The door opened a crack before widening to reveal a tall man, impeccably dressed and wearing the air of someone accustomed to being in control. "Mother, I wasn't sure you'd really come."

The mother superior stepped into the opening with a nod to Squire for him to wait for her outside. Dust danced in the sunlight streaming through the filthy paned windows and a damp mustiness permeated the air. Mildew and fish made for a rank combination. Adding the warmth of midday, it was almost more than her stomach could tolerate. Every cell in her body was on alert as it was. She certainly didn't need the nausea on top of everything else.

The man noticed her discomfort and tugged at a window sash until the warped wood gave enough for him to open it and let fresh air in. "Better?" he asked.

The nun nodded, dusted a chair off with her hand and settled her skirts as she sat. When she was comfortable, he sat across from her. She asked, "I assume you know why I wanted to see you?"

A flash of nerves gave lie to Jean-Jacques Haydel's confidence as he answered, "Haven't the faintest idea, but when the mother superior asks to see you privately, you don't turn her down."

Mother Micheaux stared at him for a long moment, before she said, "You're a damn fool, Jean."

The man leaned back and crossed his arms over his chest. He didn't take being called a fool lightly but wasn't about to challenge her. "Now, you and I both know that's not true."

"Then, you're a liar. Either way, you better start explaining about the boy."

"Boy?" he asked. The word cracked in the silence between them. Where an arrogant aristocrat sat moments before was now a frightened shell of a man. Mother Micheaux's gaze never wavered as she waited for him to start talking. Jean-Jacques' face was ashen as he searched for something, anything, that he could say to her to satisfy her. "I—I don't understand," he stammered.

"Don't you?" She slowly stood up, willing her aging back to straighten to its full height. Ramrod straight and stronger than he expected, she was a commanding figure with her long black robes and icy stare.

"N—No. I don't know what you're talking about."

She took a step towards him, and he tried to jump up out of his chair but lost his footing and ended up in the dirt on the floor. She took a step closer, then another, and another as the man scrambled backwards.

"Stop," he begged. "You don't want to do this. You know you don't." He held one hand up in front of him, as if he could deflect whatever was going to happen to him, while the other hand pushed him away from her on the floor. Heels of his boots dug ruts in the dirt.

"Then, let me fill you in." Her hand shot down in front of her, clutching at the space between them, then straight at the wall behind the man. Jean-Jacques was slammed against the wall so violently that the cabin shuddered. He hung there, a foot off the ground, kicking and screaming like a child. Hands clawed at the weathered planks behind him, leaving fingernail scratches as he tried to peel himself off. It was no use and only left him with bleeding nails and splinters. Still he tried, frantic about what the nun would do to him next.

Anger boiled in her face as she held him aloft. *"You lied to me!"* she roared. "You told me the boy was dead. You said you took care of it *yourself!*" Her rage erupted in a shower of sparks from her fingertips that burned the flesh of his face. "After everything I've given up, everything I've *done!* For *nothing!*" Mother Micheaux's hand jerked and Jean-Jacques Haydel was thrown across the room and slammed into another wall. The window beside him shattered. Tiny rivulets of blood dripped down his face where shards embedded.

Her other hand reached out into the empty space and clawed the air. His face changed from deathly pale, to red, then purple as she slowly squeezed the life from him. Sputtering against her grip, he begged for mercy. Cocking her head to the side, she threw Jean-Jacques to the ground and released him. Blood mixed with sweat streaming down his face as he gasped for air in a heap on the floor. Slow deliberate steps carried her to where he lay. Standing over him, she snarled, "Don't make me sorry I didn't kill you."

"God have mercy on your soul, you demon woman," he choked out.

"God has nothing to do with this." Calmly, she pulled a chair against the wall and sat down on it next to him. "Now, shall we try this again?"

Jean-Jacques nodded, rubbing at his throat. "What do you want?" His voice was raspy as it fought through the swelling.

"The truth, before I have to go back to New Orleans and clean up your mess."

Jean-Jacques looked up at her through heavy lids. His dark hair smeared across his sweaty forehead. Bruises formed around his neck as though her fingers had actually been there. "I told you I took care of the boy, and I did," he said through gritted teeth.

"I know what you said, but I didn't ask you to take care of him. You were supposed to clean up your nephew's mess, not ship it to Paris. My orders were for you to kill him," Mother Micheaux spat standing over him again.

"The witch would've come after me. Killed me for killing her son!" Jean-Jacques insisted.

"She could've killed you anyway, weakling. You gave her up to us. What made you think she wasn't coming for you? This is bigger than you and your precious life. Who knows how many will have to die with Julien alive? How many could've been saved with his death as a child?"

Jean-Jacques sneered. "Too holy to get your own hands dirty so you gave the chore to me. I wasn't going to have that on my soul. If you want him dead, *you* do it." Jean-Jacques pulled himself to his feet and stood eye-to-eye with the nun. His confidence and defiance were building. "I didn't bring that boy into the world. This isn't my fault.

You should have killed his mother when you had the chance. *This,*" he hissed, "is your fault."

Mother Micheaux watched him begin to pace in front of her as he gained brazenness. Energy built in her palms and held there, waiting to bring him back under her heel if she needed to. "You couldn't keep that nephew of yours under control, and you let the idiot name the boy after the family. It was bad enough she gave him the name of the one man she really loved, but you let her tie the boy to *your family.* She stole your family name! Controlling your nephew and his lust was *your* obligation. And since you couldn't do that, *you* were responsible for getting rid of the child. You're master of this plantation and the people on it. If you can't handle them, perhaps the court should give place to Marcellin after all."

Jean-Jacques snarled at her. "You wouldn't dare."

The nun's glare shifted to benign innocence. "No? You don't think so?"

"You think you're so powerful, Mother Superior, but you're out of your element on this one. You might control the souls of the court, but not the actions."

She smiled sweetly. "Gambling with your own arrogance, I see."

A sharp laugh from Jean-Jacques. His pacing stopped as his resolve wavered. "It won't work."

"Oh, it will, and I won't have to spare a drop of my own strength to do it. Let's see," Mother Micheaux said settling back into her chair. "Twenty-one years of stealing money from Marcellin, your brother and partner, sending it to France to provide for the boy so you didn't have to get your hands bloody killing the bastard. Twenty-one years of taking care of the child of a witch. What would Marcellin say if he knew where the money went? He already suspects you of fraud and wants to take the plantation. How long do you think you can hide it from him? How many more years before he has the proof he needs to destroy you? How long before someone gets angry enough to give it to him?" Her laugh was low and dark. "Well, my coward, your weakness is about to cost you more than you know."

"I won't let Marcellin take the plantation." His fists clenched at his side. "Never."

She threw back her head and laughed. It echoed off the wooden walls, rattling the splintered glass. "Do you think this is just about your precious *land*? I knew you were a fool, Jean-Jacques, but I had no idea you were this stupid." The nun held out a hand, lifting his feet off the ground, then dropping him to his knees. His face was inches from hers. "Listen to me, and listen good," she hissed. "The boy isn't in Paris, anymore. Julien's *here*. He's looking for his mother, a woman he knows as Marie Haydel. Since she can't be found in the city, his search will lead him to you." Jean-Jacques' face whitened. "And he's more like his mother than we bargained for."

"No," Jean-Jacques whispered. "You said it was just the girl. You said he wouldn't."

Mother Micheaux shook her head letting him collapse to the floor. "Perhaps you should've listened more carefully. I said *as far as we knew* the boy shouldn't. Camille didn't share her family history. All we knew about were Camille and her daughter. And the madness of her husband. There was a missing piece. Camille had a brother, Faron. A brother who was just like her, only better able to hide it."

"And the boy?"

"Has turned twenty-one and managed to annihilate an entire set of china with an angry flick of his wrist."

Jean-Jacques' hands searched for something to do as he tried to process what he was hearing, moving uncertainly from pushing his hair back to wiping at droplets of blood still seeping from the wounds on his face.

The mother superior glared at him. "How long before he realizes there *is no* Marie Haydel to find? How long before he figures out his mother is really Solène Marie Cheval?" she snapped. Jean-Jacques cringed at the name. "What happens when he finds out his mother is dead, and his sister is responsible for it? What then, Jean? I'll tell you. He'll go after Zéolie, then hunt down his father. You're the coward who let the boy live. This is *your* doing!" she growled.

"No," he muttered, pulling at his hair with trembling hands. "No, he won't find out."

A crack of laughter. "The girl can talk to her grandmother. Who says the boy won't connect with the mother he's so desperate to know? Solène could tell him *everything*. About her, about his sister, and about his father. *Your* nephew. *On your plantation.*"

"No. Julien can't come here," he groaned. Jean-Jacques' breath was coming fast and shallow as panic took over, invading every cell in his body. "He can't find his father. He can't know. But he *could* come here. He could. He *will*. He could become just like his mother! How can I lie to a monster?"

"You don't," the nun said letting his fear of what Julien might become work to her advantage. "Leave that to me," Mother Micheaux said standing and walking to the door. With her hand on the door handle, the mother superior turned to face the man one last time, letting her eyes bore into him. "You had the chance to stop all of this and you failed," she spat. "We'll handle Julien but know this —I'm not finished with you."

CHAPTER

SEVENTEEN

Julien stormed through the Quarter into the night, leaving his shattered heart in the middle of the broken glass on the Marchon's dinner table. Energy coursed through him that he couldn't understand or control. The further he got away from Zéolie, the less the electricity surged. Instead, blinding anger took its place. Rage at being rejected by the only woman he wanted consumed him, churning in his chest, as he made his way to the riverfront. Ship lights blinked lazily on the black water of the river in the dead of night, and for an instant, he thought of throwing himself into the current and riding it out to sea. Just for an instant. In the same moment, the voice that chuckled in his mind changed to a sharp gasp, startling him, before settling back into the sinister lilting laugh. The more he raged over Zéolie's rejection, the more the laugh seemed to mock him and pushed his thoughts toward the edge of madness.

Deep inside him, his blood began to surge hot and furious. Humiliation compounded his fury as he imagined the laughter of the Marchon girls when Zéolie told them how he foolishly threw himself at her.

"She let me believe I meant something to her, then threw my heart back in my face. *Damn her!*" he snarled. His hands stung as energy pooled in his fingertips. He clenched his fists, trying to ease the pain, but only succeeded in sending the energy skittering up his arms. Cold sweat gathered on his brow and upper lip despite the thick warm air. A shiver shot up his spine and back down into his feet as they fell in sharp steps.

Rumbling over the uneven street, a wagon full of crates from the warehouses passed him. Inside the crates, bottles clinked. Julien shot a look at the wagon wheel and it shattered, slamming the back corner of the cart to the ground. The horse reared as it was yanked upwards in the harness and the driver cursed as he jumped down to calm the frightened animal. Crates tumbled into the street, bursting open and spilling bottles into the gutter. Without a word, Julien stooped down, picked up a bottle of rum, and kept walking.

"You!" the driver called. "Bring that back here, thief!"

Julien slowly turned on his heel, put the cork in his mouth, and pulled it out. He spat the cork on the ground and took a slow deep drink before tossing the bottle back to the driver. As the man reached up to catch it, Julien shot his hand out in front of him, bursting the bottle over the man's head in a shower of alcohol and shards of glass. The driver stood dumbstruck as Julien put his hands in his pockets, turned around, and laughed as he walked away.

By the time he wandered to the warehouses on the waterfront, he was seething again. Dark eyes flashed dangerously at anyone who dared to look at him. The more the storm brewed inside him, the more relentless the laugh became. Only one thing had given him any relief from agony, and that was toppling the cart load and terrifying the driver. He had been in control, releasing his pain where he wanted it, and it felt good. With his emotions high from rage and humiliation, Julien searched for another release.

Past the docks, Julien found himself on Gallatin Street amid a row of ramshackle houses that seemed to be haphazardly slapped together out of whatever scrap wood the owners had managed to scrounge. A breath of air seemed enough to knock them down, and for a moment, Julien delighted at the thought before walking on. From the dilapidated buildings, music poured into the street, mixed heavily with profanity and laughter. Sailors stumbled drunk along the streets being held up by women who were as drunk as their "dates." Or at least they appeared to be. Watching one of the women pick the pocket of the man she was hanging on, Julien laughed at the charade. He could do anything he wanted, and no one would notice. On the other hand, if he shattered a bottle of rum here, it was likely to get him killed. Alcohol and women were big business on Gallatin.

A man leaned against the doorframe of one of the lopsided buildings, or it leaned against him, smoking a stump of a cigar held between his teeth as smoke curled around his face. The end glowed orange as the man pulled in another drag as Julien approached. Doing his best, which wasn't good enough, to look inconspicuous, the man used the tip of a knife blade to clean under his nails. In the glow of the cigar, Julien noticed the doorway lurker watching him.

"Evenin'," the man said through clenched teeth and cigar.

"Yes, it is," Julien returned.

The stranger stepped out of the shadow and twirled the knife between his fingers. "Party didn't go well?" the man asked taking the cigar stump out of his mouth.

Julien was startled for a second before regaining his composure. "Excuse me?"

Pointing with the tip of his blade, the man gestured to Julien's clothes. "Girls 'round here don't need ya to dress up for 'em," he laughed. "So, I'm guessin' either you're in the wrong part of town to be lookin' for a nice girl, or your party didn't go well so you came here lookin' for a good time." He looked in Julien's stormy eyes. "Judgin' from the look on your face, I'm goin' with the last one."

"Get out of my way." Julien's words were ice. The man didn't comply, but instead took a step closer, his acrid breath in Julien's face. Rage and the relentless laugh were testing his sanity, and he was losing the battle more with every passing minute, slipping deeper into his growing madness. The one thing he was beginning to understand was that relief would come, however temporary, if he released some of the building energy. The slimy idiot in front of him seemed as good a target as any. Cocking his head to one side, Julien let his mind wander about how he wanted to dispatch this new acquaintance who was foolishly challenging him. Just as Julien decided that slitting the man's throat with his own knife seemed fitting, a woman's voice called from the next doorway.

"God damnit, Arthur! You're keepin' my young man hangin' around out here. I ain't got all night."

Realizing the woman was talking about him, Julien gave a terse nod to the street thug and sidestepped him. As he did, Julien stared at the end of the knife blade the man still held out and watched it bend into a delicate curl that would shame the wrought iron galleries in the better part of the city. Arthur went pale and backed slowly away into the shadows before his footsteps were heard running down the block.

The woman winked at Julien. Several of her teeth were missing from the wide grin of crimson lipstick on her over-powdered face. Brittle reddish-blonde hair was pulled into a bun that had mostly come loose and hung down her back. Her clothes seemed to be more like bed sheets tied on with sashes than an actual dress. Straightening her posture to match the carriage of the well-dressed youth, she twisted a strand of hair around one of her fingers and rested her other hand on an ample hip. As he watched her twirling her hair, she reminded him in a sick way of Celeste Marchon.

"Don't let Arthur get to ya," she said. "The damned men here like to pretend they run things."

"And they don't?" Julien asked.

The woman snorted. "Hell, no. It's the women you need to watch out for."

Julien narrowed his eyes. "Oh?"

"Well," she laughed, "some of 'em. Most of us would rather our customers came back and spent more money. Only the stupid ones or the crazy ones'll rob 'em and kill 'em."

"And how are the men supposed to know which is which?" Julien asked, enjoying the conversation with the harlot.

With another wink, she said, "That's part of the excitement, now, ain't it?" Looping her arm through his, she went on, "The way I see it, I got rid of Arthur for ya, so you owe me."

"I'd say putting your neck out there is worth a drink."

She pouted. "You can do better than that."

"No, and I don't actually have to do that much. So, is it a drink, or do I keep walking?" Julien asked.

"I'm starting to think you didn't need my help after all," she laughed. "Name's Nora Finnegan. A drink it is. Come on in." She led Julien into the parlor of the brothel and past the jealous stares of the girls with their rougher dates. Most of the women wore clothes that were threadbare and loose, and like Nora's, were held on mostly with sashes and cords. In various states of undress with their customers, all of the girls were completely distracted by him. A couple of them winked, or ran their tongues across their lips, but they all gave Nora a wide berth. It didn't take Julien long to realize the woman he was with was the madam.

Lamplight glowed in the middle of the room on small side tables next to battered wooden chairs, likely stolen at some point from one of the bars. In darkened corners, softer chairs were occupied by men with girls in their laps. The walls were covered in a faded rose brocade wallpaper he was certain Nora must have traded services for. As shabby as it was, it was nicer than anything else in the house. On the far wall was a cabinet that had been turned into a makeshift bar. Below soot stains on the pink brocade on either side of the bar, lamps were burning brightly, probably so Nora had a well-lit view of the only commodity in the place more expensive than the girls.

"Nice place," he said as she handed him a drink. He tossed Nora a few coins which she shoved into cleavage made full by a well-tied sash.

"It's a hell hole," she answered, "but it's *my* hell hole." Sitting in the chair across from him, she lit a cigarette and crossed her legs, letting the bedsheet dress slide off her thigh. "So, Paris, what brings *you* to my hell hole?"

"Paris?" Julien asked.

"Sure. There's just enough French in your accent and enough taste to your clothes to let me know you're not from New Orleans. Paris, I'd say, by the arrogance."

"Fair enough," Julien said, trying to pay more attention to the woman across from him than the couple behind her making full use of the stability of the armchair.

"So, what's her name?" Nora asked.

"Whose?"

"The girl who broke your heart. We get the sailors off the boats all the time, and the fat aristocrats bored with their wives, but when the handsome young ones find their way to Gallatin Street, it's heartbreak."

"Her name doesn't matter," Julien said, sipping the whiskey. It was cheap and harsh, but he didn't care. "All that matters is that she doesn't love me like I love her."

Nora leaned back and sighed. "I'll never understand women. Men, well, they're easy. A wink, a smile, a toss of the head, and they'll fall in love. I figure that's what happened to you. Women, god only knows what they're thinkin'."

Julien laughed. "I'd have thought you'd be sort of an expert on women."

Nora snorted again. "Hell, no. Not decent ones anyway. These girls are interested in one thing, so they're easy enough to understand."

"Sex?"

"Jesus, no. Money, my handsome one. Money." She ran a finger around the rim of her glass. "They make enough to keep themselves alive, but it's no real life."

"Seems like you'd get enough business to do pretty well here."

"If everyone who walked in had your money, we'd all be happy and rich. No, what we get is poor starved sailors, scum like Arthur after they've managed to rip off someone like you, and police we owe favors to." Nora tossed back the end of her whiskey. "Hell, even if they made a decent living, these girls wouldn't live long enough to spend it."

"What do you mean?" Julien asked.

"Ever seen an old whore? No. This life'll kill ya before ya get a single gray hair on your head."

Julien watched Nora intently as she talked about her line of work and the list of things likely to do her girls in, focusing on Nora's emotions and thoughts. She had no love for the life she led or the women who worked for her. Her ambitions were higher. The brothel was a means to an end for her. Nora Finnegan may not have known any old whores, but she was determined she'd live to be an old madam. Lurking under her pleasant exterior was a ruthless businesswoman. This, Julien decided, was something he could use.

If he was able to shatter glass, splinter wagon wheels, and bend knife blades when he wanted to, then maybe he could use that same power on people. A content chuckle from the depths of his mind floated to the surface at the thought. To find out, he'd need to figure out how to harness and direct the energy that constantly begged for release. Zéolie didn't love him tonight, but there had to be a way he could take the love he wanted. Make her love him. He didn't know how to do it, though, and Zéolie's own impenetrable mind could be a challenge. If he wanted to take Zéolie, then he'd need women to practice on. Ones that wouldn't be missed if things went wrong. With enough money, and just the right amount of fear, the amiable and ruthless Gallatin Street madam could be a valuable asset.

"Nora, take a walk with me."

CHAPTER

EIGHTEEN

Tension dripped down the walls of the house on Dauphine Street. Shadows crept in corners, fearing the sunlight stealing in from the edges of the drapes drawn tight against the day. The house held its breath as the two women inside set to work.

Zéolie sent Lucien and Alida to the Marchons to visit their daughter who was Lisette's maid so she and the priestess would have the house to themselves. Keeping the ritual away from prying eyes was one reason for sending them away, but she had selfish reasons, too. She knew Alida would be full of news from the Marchon women that she would be only too eager to share with her new mistress. In the meantime, there was work to do.

"First, we're goin' to cleanse this house, then you're comin' back to the convent," the priestess said as she gathered supplies for the ritual.

Zéolie glowered at her. "I don't need to be looked after like an invalid anymore. I can take care of myself."

Mama Nell stood in front of her, feet planted. "You'll come, and I don' want to hear anythin' else about it."

"No," Zéolie said shaking her dark head defiantly. "I can't just hide from him. He was upset because I turned him down. Heartbroken. He won't hurt me if he loves me."

"You can't count on that. An' until we know more 'bout what's goin' on with that boy, you need to be invisible. Now, we got work to do here. Enough of this." Zéolie sulked but didn't push the argument anymore.

In the center of the foyer floor, Mama Nell crouched in front of a bucket of water. Beside her lay two rags.

Next to those was a chamber pot. Zéolie stood with her arms crossed at her waist and her face wrinkled in disgust but said nothing. Far be it from her to question the methods of the priestess when it came to protecting her house. Using a tin cup, Mama Nell dipped urine from the chamber pot and poured it into the bucket of water. Over and over, she did this chanting in her rich sing-song voice those words Zéolie had come to know. Finished, the priestess stood with the chamber pot in her hand holding it out for Zéolie to take. "Toss what's left out the back door toward the gate, then come back and help me with this."

Zéolie did as she was told and came back into the foyer to find her aunt dipping a rag into the water and scrubbing the front door with it in long methodical strokes from the top down. "What are you doing?" she asked.

"Spirits tend to get in through doors, windows, and other openin's. Scrub 'em with this and they won't want to pass through."

"Neither would I."

"There, see?" Mama Nell said handing Zéolie the other rag. "You do the window frames. Get the sill good, too. Careful not to move the curtains too much. We don' want to draw attention to the fact you're home."

Repulsed, but obedient, Zéolie dipped the rag into the pungent water and washed down the window as Nell chanted. Meticulously, they worked through every opening in the house from the inside from the bottom to the top and front to back. Dried sage leaves smoldered in bowls in each of the rooms as much to soften the odor as to calm any malevolent spirits that might already be inside. In each windowsill, Mama Nell placed a small black stone as she opened the window slightly to give the spirits running from her cleansing a way out of the house. Ground floor windows were barely open, but the upstairs windows were opened wider.

The spiritual cleansing continued next with the floors. Beginning at the rear of the house on the second floor, the priestess took the remaining water from the bucket and poured more water in. In the mortar and pestle, she crushed salt rocks with a clove of garlic until it was a fine paste. Then, she stirred that into the water with a stick. To keep the garlic from overwhelming, she measured Florida Water into a shot glass. The citrus and floral scents of the cologne masked some, but not all of the harsher odors in the wash. She and Zéolie each took a brush, dipped it into the bucket and scrubbed from the rear of the rooms, towards the doors, and down the stairs. On the ground floor, they began from the back door in the same way until they reached the front door.

"Now," Mama Nell said dropping her brush into the bucket, "we get this away from the house to throw it out. We don't want any lingerin' bad energy let loose too close to here after all that work."

"Where do we take it?" Zéolie asked. Her mother's laugh had echoed through her mind as she worked, making her wonder if all of this was enough to protect them from what she knew was possible. When she first heard the laugh, it seemed distant and disconnected. Lately, it was more real, more like it had been when her mother was taunting her. This cleansing had to work to keep that madness from infecting her and her house again.

"I don't want to open the door and jus' go walkin' out there. For all we know, Julien's watchin' the house. We'll take it all with us in the carriage later and toss it far from the house and you."

Zéolie nodded. "Now what do we do?"

"Smoke out any evil still lurkin' in here."

With a nod to the parlor, Nell glided through the doorway in a rustling of skirts and scarves. Gingerly, she lifted the woven basket from its place by the fireplace and set it on the small round table Zéolie used for seances. For a moment, her fingers traced the fibers of the basket lovingly. Zéolie knew her aunt was thinking of her lost love, Vernand, and gave her a moment with her memory.

With a slight smile and the glistening of a tear on her long lashes, Mama Nell lifted the white cloth to reveal the contents. At the bottom of the basket was a small cast iron bowl on a chain. Nell held a long match from the fireplace to a small lump of charcoal, letting it pop and hiss as it caught the flame. Dropping it into the bowl, she watched it smolder before sprinkling on remnants of the garlic from the mortar and pestle.

"Put a handkerchief over your mouth an' nose for this next part," the priestess instructed. She did the same, then sprinkled dried cayenne onto the garlic and charcoal. The pepper in the air stung their eyes, but the cloth kept the women from inhaling the vapors and choking on them.

Wrapping a cloth around her hand, she picked up the chain that ran through each of the small loops on either side and carried the bowl to the corner of the room as the smoke rose. "There's a crow's feather in that basket. Use it to fan the smoke where I tell ya," Mama Nell instructed from behind her handkerchief. Zéolie dug in the basket and produced the ink black feather. Turning it in her hand, it glistened in what little light was seeping into the room. "Now," the priestess said, "fan the smoke deep into the corners. We don't want anythin' lingerin' there." Once again, room by room, they purged the house with smoke.

Thick haze filled the house as the priestess finished the cleansing. Smoke curled and danced on the air current from the windows before sliding out through the openings, ideally taking the malevolent spirits with it. Through the cloud, Zéolie asked. "Is that it?"

Mama Nell winked at her niece. "No, *chérie*, we just gettin' started. We cleaned the place out, but now we got to protect it." The priestess sat at the table and motioned for Zéolie to sit with her.

"The ingredients for purgin' and protectin' aren't much different. We start with more salt and cayenne."

"Why is it that magic seems a lot like cooking?" Zéolie asked.

Mama Nell chuckled. "How do you know it's not that cookin' is a lot like magic?"

Pouring a mound of pepper on the table, the priestess took the silver blade from her hip pocket and began drawing sigils in it. Each delicate magical symbol poured her intent into the powder. Once the sigils were drawn, she pulled a cigar from somewhere in all the scarves at her waist and bit off the end. "Can you get me a match?" she asked.

Zéolie went to the fireplace and pulled a long matchstick from the box beside the mantle and set it on the table. Using the rough edge of a piece of quartz crystal, Mama Nell lit the match and let it burn down to the wood before putting it to the end of the cigar. Holding it between clenched teeth, she pulled at the flame until the tobacco burned and the rich smoke bathed her face.

Like she had done with Zéolie when she cleansed her for the ritual to contact Camille, Mama Nell pushed smoke through the end of the cigar onto the pepper and sigils. Between puffs, she chanted her intention for the spice to consecrate it to its purpose. Somewhere in all the chanting, Zéolie noticed the words changed from Mama Nell's own to more familiar words. The words of the 91st Psalm, but not in the Latin she was accustomed to hearing it. This time, the words were familiar and personal, not cold and recited.

Zéolie lost herself in the words of the prayer of protection. "...No evil will touch you, neither will plague come to your house, for he will send his angels to you, to protect you in all your ways...You'll tread upon the lion and the snake: the young lion and the dragon you'll trample under your feet..."

The young lion and the dragon... The words reverberated in her head with the echo of her mother's laugh, but why?

The psalm finished, Mama Nell set the cigar in the cast iron bowl with the charcoal to burn itself out. Standing, she swept the pepper into the palm of her hand. "Take some of this, too, and you can help me," the priestess said. She poured some of it into Zéolie's open hand then led her around to every doorway in the house. Across each one, they sprinkled the pepper. "Now, each time anybody comes through the door, this'll stop their negative energy."

What little light came through the heavy curtains began to fade from deep orange to a silvery gray as the sun sank behind the buildings of the Quarter. Once the thresholds were protected, there was only one step left. Cleansing themselves. "It's your house and the energy is goin' to be drawn most to you. Time to wash it away."

The walk to the kitchen across the courtyard was refreshing after the oppression of the smoke-filled house. Zéolie breathed deep and walked slowly behind her aunt, enjoying the cooling night air before going into the heat of the kitchen. Hanging over the coals was a large pot of water, steaming and heating gently. One at a time, Mama Nell began sprinkling herbs from glass jars lining the kitchen shelves into the pot. Rosemary, salt, hyssop, and rue. After letting the herbs steep in the water for a few seconds, she swung the pot away from the coals on the iron arm that held it aloft.

"Now, we wash the negative away."

"What do we do?" Zéolie asked.

"Strip."

"Excuse me?"

"Take those clothes off so we can bathe you."

Zéolie peeled layers of clothes off, piling them into a corner of the kitchen. The heat that was oppressive minutes before was blessedly welcome as she stood naked near the fire. Dipping a cup into the warm water, Mama Nell began pouring it over Zéolie's head letting it run down her face, coating her in herbal purity.

Cup after cup, the water washed over her, taking any clinging negativity with it as it trickled down her bare skin to the kitchen floor. Bits of green rosemary leaves, purple hyssop flowers, and yellow rue clung to her wet skin that glistened in the firelight. Zéolie's long black hair clung to her back and shoulders, dripping down her breasts. Steam rose as the heat dried her where she stood before the next cupful cascaded over her. Finally, the last of the water ran down her body into the puddle on the floor at her feet.

"Stay here and let the fire dry you. I'll get you some clothes," Mama Nell said.

"What about you? Don't you need a bath, too?" Zéolie asked.

Mama Nell nodded. "We'll get you dressed while another pot heats."

Dressed again, Zéolie began the ritual cleansing of Mama Nell, who stood with her back to her niece, arms crossed across her chest and caramel hands resting just under her shoulders. As the scented water was poured over her head, it beaded in her tight reddish curls before streaming down her skin. After a few cups, the priestess' hair was soaked enough to pull straight down to the middle of her strong, graceful back. Flower petals and herb leaves clung to her hair and skin as Zéolie continued the spiritual bath.

Moonlight splashed across the courtyard, sending shadows through the garden by the time the women completed the cleansing and protection rituals. Hair still damp, Zéolie pulled it into a braid as Mama Nell wrung hers out and wrapped it into a clean tignon. Cleansed and dry, the two women leaned in the kitchen doorway as a carriage pulled up to the *porte-cochère*. Seconds later, there was a patterned knock on the gate.

"Stay out of sight, jus' in case" the priestess said. Zéolie nodded and her aunt went to open it.

Mother Micheaux's carriage backed into the courtyard, ready to quickly leave again if necessary. The carriage door opened, and Louis swung down. Zéolie rushed to him falling into his open arms. Pushing a lock of damp dark hair away from her face, he pressed his lips to hers and lifted her onto her toes. "It felt good enough just to be out of that room, but this," he said kissing her forehead, "feels even better."

"What are you doing here?" Zéolie asked settling her head onto his chest. His strength and warmth surrounded her heart as he held her.

Louis exchanged a look with Mama Nell. "You didn't tell her?"

"I did, but she won't listen to me."

"I appreciate the concern, but really, I can take care of myself." Zéolie said.

Mama Nell shook her head. "You're not as strong as you think you are, *chérie*. Together is safer right now. Besides, you haven't got your strength back yet."

"I'm certainly not helpless, and I've got more power than I let on. I just don't want to risk losing control of it," Zéolie insisted.

Irritated with not being listened to, Mama Nell's patience ran thin. "She'll be back soon, and we won't be there when she does. We got no time to argue about this."

The more Zéolie resisted and insisted on her strength, the more insistent her mother's laugh became. Frustrated, she broke away from Louis and paced.

"Nell, could you give us a few minutes alone, please?" Louis asked.

"Fine," throwing her hands in the air, exasperated with her niece.

Louis stood for a moment watching Nell go into the kitchen before he approached Zéolie slowly. "*Chérie*," he began gently, "no one is saying you can't take care of yourself, but we don't even know what you're up against. All we want is for you to stay out of danger until we have more answers. Answers that can help you direct the power you have where and when you need it most."

Zéolie stopped her pacing and dropped her head. "I know you mean well, but it just makes me feel so...weak. I can't be weak. Camille sent me back here to finish something and weakness isn't an option."

Louis smiled down at her and wrapped his arms around Zéolie's waist. "No one thinks you're weak, *chérie*. When it's time, you'll be able to do whatever it is you need to. But until we know what that is, we need to be smart about this." Louis put his finger under her chin and lifted it, looking into her eyes. "I love you more than you can ever know. Please come back with me. Do this for me. Please."

Zéolie softened into Louis' embrace as his lips found hers. In that moment, she wanted everything to fade away. Julien, her mother's laugh, everything but Louis. "Alright," Zéolie said as he pulled away looking at her expectantly. "But only because I love you."

Louis' eyes twinkled as he grinned down at her. "Nell," he called toward the kitchen, "we're going!"

CHAPTER

NINETEEN

"Where is she?" Zéolie moaned as she paced the floor under the convent. "She should've been back by now."

"Stop that pacin', *chérie*, and drink your tea," Mama Nell ordered. "Wearin' yourself out with worry won't get 'er here any faster." Zéolie huffed, but obediently sat in the chair in front of the steaming cup her aunt set down. Mama Nell set another cup in front of Louis. "You, too, Louis."

He reluctantly left his post by the door where he had been listening for Mother Micheaux's footsteps on the stairs. "Can't you put something in it to make it taste better?" he asked as he sat down.

Zéolie saw the blue lines of his veins even through the dirty blonde stubble on his cheeks. Except for the paleness and map of veins under his skin, he, like Zéolie, showed no sign of his resurrection.

"You two go on like a couple of children!" Mama Nell scolded. "Like any good medicine, the nastier it is, the better it works. Now, hush and drink it."

The two of them obediently drank the swamp water tea, silently grumbling about it as the priestess crushed herbs in the mortar and

128

pestle to make another batch for later. Zéolie wanted to know what was in it, but every time she asked, she was reminded of the reason for the secret. "If anyone ever found out what was keepin' you strong, they could sabotage it," Nell had cautioned. "It's your mind they'll be in, whoever they are, and if you don't know, neither do they."

As Zéolie drained the last of the tea from her cup, she heard the familiar sound of metal scraping metal in the door lock. Her eyes met Louis' for a moment, apprehensive about what the nun would say, but anxious for answers. The door opened slowly and Mother Micheaux stepped through it, covered in dust from the long ride. Horsehair still clung to her black skirts and shimmers in the lamplight revealed tiny bits of glass stuck in the fabric. Whatever she had learned on her trip couldn't even wait for her to change robes.

"Mother! Are you alright?" Louis said, jumping up to help her, knocking his chair over in the process.

The mother superior waved him away. "I'm fine, Louis, thank you. I just need to sit on something other than that damned saddle." Louis picked his chair up, set it back on its legs, and offered it to the nun. "Thank you," she said again.

Mama Nell poured her a drink. "What happened?"

Mother Micheaux threw back the shot of rum and looked at the three of them. How could she tell them what she knew? How could she tell them she could have headed it all off years ago if she'd only been strong enough? "Before I tell you what I know, I need you to understand that I did what I thought was best at the time. Please, understand that," she pleaded.

Zéolie knelt at the mother superior's feet and took her thin wrinkled hand. "We've all made mistakes. Whatever it is, I"—she looked at the expectant faces of Mama Nell and Louis—"*we* will understand it as best we can." Zéolie gave her hand a gentle squeeze. "What happened?"

"Years ago, when your father banished your mother, we were so focused on protecting you that we didn't do enough to contain

Solène. I don't know what her motives were. Maybe she was lonely, but more likely it was revenge against the man who left her. After she was taken to the cabin, Nell's mother worked on her wounds and soon she was stronger than any of us realized. One night—" Mother Micheaux stopped and glanced at Mama Nell, who nodded even with tears in her beautiful green eyes. "One night, she overpowered Nell's mother—" tears streamed down Nell's face. "Her mother was a powerful priestess, but Solène was stronger. Strong, angry, and insane. In a blind rage at having her life and love stripped from her, Solène killed Nell's mother and escaped.

"By the time any of us knew what happened, she vanished. Soon, word came through slave gossip from St. John Parrish about finding strange things in the woods and fields. Dead animals stripped of their skins, symbols in the dirt around remains of campfires, trinkets hung in the trees. Before the rumors made it to those of us who knew what was happening, Jean-Jacques Haydel sent men into the woods to find out what was going on. His suspicion was escaped slaves trying to curse his plantation. He was wrong."

"Solène," Louis said. The police officer in him listened to every detail of the story, putting it together a beat before Zéolie.

Mother Micheaux nodded. "One of the men sent out to search was the young nephew of Jean-Jacques. He didn't find any escaped slave, but he did find a beautiful woman with raven hair. Solène seduced him, easily I imagine, and before long, he was spending more time in her camp in the woods than at the plantation. By the time Jean-Jacques found out, she was heavy with child."

Louis' eyes widened. "No. It can't be," he whispered. He looked at Zéolie to see if she'd put it together, too. Her white face told him she had.

"Julien," she said. The word quivered.

The mother superior closed her eyes and nodded. The story pained her to tell, and she knew it couldn't be easy for Zéolie to hear. "The young Haydel challenged his uncle who threatened to kill Solène for the witch she was. Jean-Jacques couldn't bring himself to duel against his nephew and knew Solène would kill him if he did. Solène threatened him with the lives of everyone on the plantation if he gave her away, knowing we'd be looking for her, but once the child was born, her madness became more than he could take. He feared her and her spawn, so he sent word to Father Antoine and me.

"We knew the two of us couldn't take her without help."

Zéolie turned flashing dark eyes on the priestess. "You knew all along? You knew who Julien was and you didn't tell me?"

Mama Nell held up a hand to stop her tirade. "Yes, but until we knew for sure—"

"How could you *not know*? How many Julien Haydel's could there possibly be?" Zéolie shot back.

"I'm so sorry, *chérie*, but I had to know for sure."

Louis put his arms around Zéolie, who trembled with anger and betrayal. "I know you're angry, but I'm sure she had her reasons." Brushing a strand of dark hair from her face, he kissed her softly on the forehead. "Go on, Mother."

The nun nodded and continued, "Nell, Vernand, and your father rode out with us."

"My father?" Zéolie gasped, pulling away from Louis.

Mama Nell took over the story from the emotion-weary nun. "Your father was the only one who ever had any control over your mama. If we had any hope of overpowerin' her, we'd need one hell of a distraction. We knew we'd have maybe a few good seconds while Solène got over her shock at seein' him. It'd have to be enough."

Louis shook his head and asked, "How did you know she wouldn't try to kill him after what he did to her?"

"We didn't," Mama Nell answered. "And Julien knew it, too. He knew if she was loose, she'd come for his baby girl, and if it cost him his life to protect Zéolie, it was a risk he'd take."

A sob rocked Zéolie, and she collapsed into Louis' chest again. He held her tight and rubbed her back, letting her cry. Mama Nell and Mother Micheaux dabbed at their own tears as she broke down.

After a few minutes, Zéolie looked up at Louis with glistening eyes and tear-stained cheeks. "I'm alright."

Louis kissed her forehead again and said to the two older women, "What happened?"

Mother Micheaux continued. "We got exactly what we hoped for. Jean-Jacques made sure his nephew was at the main house when we got there so he wouldn't get caught in the crossfire of Solène's fury, but he didn't have the guts to take her baby from her."

"How did you get close to her without her knowing?" Zéolie asked. Her mother had been able to infiltrate her thoughts. Surely, she could have sensed the strange army coming for her.

The mother superior shook her head. "Honestly, I don't know. Part of me thinks she knew we were coming, but was confident enough that she could overpower us, but her reaction to Julien makes me think she had no idea. With us in the tree line near where she lived, Julien walked into her camp alone. It was little more than a small clearing in the woods. She'd constructed a hut from branches and cloth she'd greased to keep out the rain. Coals smoldered near the door with some small animal roasting on a spit. Skins were stretched and drying against the shack wall. In a pot on the edge of the coals, there was an animal boiling in water. A film of fat coated the top of the liquid as the carcass bobbed in the water. It wasn't until we got closer, I realized it was a cat. In the low branches around the camp, she'd hung talismans and charms. Small dolls with odds and ends pinned to them, feathers bound to animal bones, and bundles of herbs. As strange as it was to see her living in the woods, she seemed perfectly at home there.

"Solène was singing to the baby and dancing with him. She turned, saw her husband standing there, and went white. Clutching the baby to her chest, she trembled and began backing away. Julien knew that as long as she held the child, she'd be distracted. He talked to her so gently that she stopped her retreat. Solène was visibly torn between running to Julien and running away from him, so she did neither. He watched her face for any sign of attack as he inched his way to her, talking to her to hold her attention. He knew that as long as she was focused on him, we could get into position to take her down.

"Julien slowly reached a hand out and pulled the cloth away from the baby's face to look at him. That was more than Solène could take. She started shrieking at him about stealing her little girl and how she'd die before he took her baby boy. We only had seconds to react. Julien took the child and knocked her to the ground. Father Antoine and I held her while Nell forced a sleeping drug down her throat. But not before taking a burst of energy from the raging witch."

Mama Nell pulled the neckline of her loose white top down to reveal the edge of a nasty scar in the hollow between her breasts. Her rich caramel skin was shiny and rippled where the energy had burned her all those years ago. "She managed jus' that one shot before she went out," the priestess said. "We were lucky. If it wasn't for your father—"

"What happened to the child?" Louis asked Mother Micheaux. "To Julien?"

"We took Solène back to the cabin. Using my father's books and every trick she knew, Nell was able to contain her for the time being. While we went ahead, Julien brought his namesake to the Haydel's with instructions to take care of him until I returned. Days later, I went back to the plantation with orders for Jean-Jacques." She paused and took a deep breath. Telling the painful memories was taking its toll on her. More tears began to shimmer on her gray eyelashes. "Zéolie, please understand, we were frightened and only trying to keep you and your father safe. We knew what she was and had no idea what would happen with you. We couldn't take the risk of her coming for the boy. Alone, she was something we could contain. If he grew up and could help her, we were afraid she'd become stronger than we could handle."

Zéolie stared at the nun. "What did you tell Jean-Jacques Haydel when you saw him?" It was an empty question. She knew the answer.

Mother Micheaux dropped her eyes and a tear fell onto the wrinkled hand that clutched her rosary. "I told him to kill the child." Whispered words with the power to tear the mother superior apart. "I had to," she said looking up at Zéolie, pleading with her to understand. "She couldn't have him, and we knew she wouldn't stop fighting us until she had Julien back."

"Why didn't you do the same thing to him that you did for me?"

"We tried. But there was a difference. Your father was willing to put his life on the line to protect you and take the risk with whatever you became. The boy's father refused. He was young and stupid, and whatever spell Solène had him under was broken when we took her away. Jean-Jacques wanted nothing to do with the witch or her child and tried to get me to take him. Knowing the force the child was tied to, I couldn't bring him here, and I couldn't let anyone else adopt him. It would be sentencing innocent people to death if Solène found out. At the time, there seemed to be only one option."

"Then why let me live?" Zéolie asked. "You didn't know Julien would inherit her powers or her madness. Or both. You *knew* the power was passed through the women. You knew I'd become what she was."

The mother superior trembled under the weight of her emotions. "Even if your father would've done it, we knew Solène would destroy all of us, and god knows who else, if she knew her daughter—the one she knew for sure would inherit her power—was taken from her. As long as you lived, we knew she'd have to wait out the years with you under our protection until you came of age. It bought us time. Julien's life was only a liability, especially since none of us thought he would inherit her powers. There was no age to reach. She could come for him at any time. Julien alive tied Solène to an innocent family. Killing him would spare them from her if she managed to get herself free."

"Wait," Louis said, "wouldn't she be angry at them for killing her baby? Seems like protecting the boy would have been safer, even if it would've tied her to them."

Mama Nell stepped in. "You may be right. And she could've come for 'em for givin' her up to us. Either way, their lives were put on the line the minute young Haydel fell for 'er. Besides, it's easy to make different choices when we look back, and when the panic doesn't cloud judgement."

"I'm sorry, I didn't mean—" Louis muttered. "I don't know what I would've done."

"It doesn't matter now," Mother Micheaux said. Exhaustion draped itself heavily on her shoulders, bending them under its weight. "Jean was a fool and a liar. He said he'd take care of the boy and that's exactly what he did, even if it wasn't the way I ordered.

"Solène managed another escape, this time less violently. Circumventing the power holding her, she slipped into the swamp. We searched but couldn't find her. She just—just vanished."

Zéolie's brows knit. "That can't be right. Julien said he'd known his mother but was very young when he was sent away from her."

Mother Micheaux looked at Mama Nell, then slowly turned to Zéolie. "What did you say?"

"He said he'd known his mother, but it was so long ago he didn't even remember what she looked like. The night you took him away from her wasn't the last time he saw her."

Confusion turned to rage as the nun processed what she was told. "That bastard Haydel lied to me," she seethed. "We searched there. Jean-Jacques was hiding her *and* the child! *Damn him!*"

Louis paced the floor as he thought. "That means he likely was hiding her for years, keeping her just far enough away to keep his family safe. How else would she have survived on her own? She was getting food, clothes, supplies from somewhere. It had to be Jean-Jacques."

"She wouldn't kill the man protecting and providing for her, so that bought him safety," Zéolie said picking up the thread of reasoning. "And security might have been enough motivation for letting him send Julien to Paris."

Mother Micheaux nodded. "I guess even the maddest of mothers can still want the best for their children."

"But what we don't know," Louis continued, "is how much of Solène is in Julien. We know he has her power, but to what degree? And how much control of it?"

"An' was his outburst anger alone," Mama Nell asked, "or is the boy as mad as his mother?"

Mother Micheaux lowered her head. "That, I'm afraid, is something we may not know until it's too late."

CHAPTER

TWENTY

J ulien once again found himself standing in the swamp watching flames consuming the cypress trees. In front of him, the cabin on stilts looked precarious at best. Firelight shimmered on the wet boggy ground and steam hissed. He'd been here so many nights, the nightmare was beginning to feel familiar.

This time, though, something was different, but he struggled to figure out what. There were the same sights, sounds, smells. That wasn't it. Something just felt different.

Turning slowly, Julien watched the edges of the scene come more into focus than they ever had. Instead of jumping from image to image in manic flashes, it held steady. What was usually hollow and disconnected began to feel strangely real. No longer was he on the outside looking in at an unfamiliar place. He was deep inside it. And he wasn't alone. Somewhere, there was someone watching him. Someone he couldn't see or sense the thoughts of, but he could feel them.

"Very good, *chérie*," a woman's voice said echoing around him. He'd heard it before, laughing. "You're getting stronger if you can feel me."

"Who are you? *Where* are you?" Julien asked. He spun, searching the edges of the woods for the woman but couldn't see anything except dancing flames.

"Patience, *chérie*. Not yet, my love. Soon. When you're ready."

The words echoed as the images around him began to feel hollow again and fade. "Wait!" he called into the vacuum. "Don't go!" Julien didn't know why he wanted the voice to come back. He didn't even know who she was. "Do you know what's happening to me?" he shouted.

"Yes, *chérie*. You're *mine*," the voice said sweetly. It was barely there. A shimmering whisper of words, but he was certain he'd heard them.

Frustration began to build as he searched the emptiness. "I don't understand!" he called. "Please!" No images. No words. Nothing.

As he struggled to get his bearings, Zéolie's face was once more in front of him, smiling warmly. His heart leaped in his chest, aching for her. Dark eyes inches from him, silken black hair wild and loose, and her crooked smile full of mischief. Julien tried to reach for her, to touch her pale face, but as he did, her smile changed from playful to mocking. Laughter spilled from her beautiful lips, but not sweet and joyful. No, she was laughing at him. Laughing at the love he tried to give her and his foolishness.

Anger surged where love had been. Red blinding rage. Before Julien realized what he was doing, his hand flew up to slap her. As his palm met her white cheek, she evaporated, leaving only her ringing laughter. But it wasn't hers alone. Another voice chuckled under the remnants of Zéolie's.

Music drifted over the rooftops, giving a pulse to the night. Julien woke to the evening sounds of the French Quarter and a throbbing headache. The day had slipped past in fitful dreams that danced along the edge of nightmare, and the evening brought only confusion. Staring at the ceiling in Madame Fontaine's boarding house, he grappled with reality.

In the purgatory between sleep and waking, there were memories that seemed disconnected, yet intertwined so tightly he struggled to decipher what was real and what was dreamt. Julien's fractured mind assembled the pieces of the past night, turning them over slowly, until the memories slid into place. The image they created sickened him as it came into focus.

"What have I done?" Julien groaned. He had no answer. With every passing day, he'd felt more like he was on the outside looking in on his own life. Reality seemed thin and fragile, as though it was weary from keeping up a charade.

A woman's voice chuckled somewhere deep inside him, then began to sing. Julien strained to hear the words, but they were so faint, he could only make out the tune. It was simple and familiar, but he couldn't place it. He knew that voice, though. She had spoken to him last night. Soft and sweet. He didn't understand why, but rather than being unnerved by it, he clung to the voice like a precious memory.

"Who are you?" he asked. "Can you hear me?" A gentle laugh, then the singing resumed. It was enough. He knew she could hear him, whoever she was, and last night he could feel her as if she was standing next to him. *But why?*

Leaving the question in the air, Julien rolled over in the bed and saw the glass on the floor, lifeless and dull in the fading dusk. Holding his palm out toward the pieces, he raised his hand slightly. Splintered glass lifted on a ripple of energy, hovering just above the floorboards. A slight bend of his fingers and the glass waved on the current. Lifting his hand higher, the glass followed.

"I know I can destroy things," he muttered. "Let's see if I can fix things, too." Closing his eyes, he pictured the hurricane lamp globe that the shards were before. Opening his eyes and twisting his wrist, he spun the pieces into a vortex that slowly began to fuse together. Gently, he lifted the glass over the base of the lamp and set the solidifying globe down on the brass ring. A flick of his fingers, and a flame danced on the wick. "Well," he said, "I guess there's hope for me yet." The low laugh in his mind seemed amused at the thought.

As quietly as he could so not to arouse the curiosity of his landlady, Julien got up and dressed. Nora Finnegan would be waiting for him, but first, he needed to set things right with Zéolie. She may not love him, but he had to at least find a way to keep her close if he was ever going to have her. Without a sound, he slipped out the back door and into the night, the voice softly serenading him all the while.

GAS LANTERNS FLICKERED in their cages illuminating the plaster of the house on Dauphine Street. Julien glanced up at the balcony with a fleeting hope Zéolie'd be there with a bottle of wine once more but was disappointed. Other than the lamps by the front door, the house was dark.

Nerves that had twisted his gut on the walk through the Quarter began to unravel as he stood feet away from her steps. Tingling fingers opened and closed, deciding whether or not to knock. Electricity in his body and mind surged and ebbed like a psychotic tide, clouding his thoughts and judgement. Common sense told him to turn around and vanish into the night, to run to Nora and Gallatin Street where freaks and demons like him walked hand in hand, but his feet wouldn't listen to reason.

Before he had a chance to approach the door, voices floated on the evening breeze from the courtyard behind the house. Two voices were unfamiliar, but one belonged to his soul. Zéolie. His heart pounded in his ears—louder, louder, and louder—with every step toward the side of the house and the *porte-cochère*. Standing in front of the gate, he could hardly hear the voices over the sound of his heartbeat. He wanted to shut out the noise, but he couldn't quiet the beating any more than he could stop the lullaby in his head. The two together reverberated inside his skull, driving him to distraction. *No,* he thought, *not now. Please, stop this madness.* It was no use. The cacophony crescendoed as he stood in the shadows with only pieces of the courtyard conversation breaking through the noise.

"—she won't listen to me—" Creole voice with a Haitian lilt.

"—can take care of myself—" Zéolie.

"—not as strong as you think you are, *cherie*—" Creole.

"—not helpless—more power than I let on—" Zéolie. *Power? What does that mean?*

"—she'll be back soon—no time to argue—" Creole.

"—a few minutes alone—" Male voice.

"Fine." Creole and fading footsteps.

Voices whispering under the din of pounding and wordless singing.

Then, male voice, "—do this for me. Please." *Do what?*

Pause. "Alright." Zéolie. "But only because I love you."

The world crashed down on Julien where he stood, knocking the wind out of him. Jagged pieces of his heart tore at his insides, ripping him to shreds. Inside his mind, the voice stopped singing and shrieked with laughter as the pounding reached a fever-pitch. Trembling hands on fire with energy covered his ears as he sank down against the wall, struggling to keep control and losing the battle. Fingernails dug into his scalp and rivulets of blood trickled down his knuckles.

Male voice. "Nell, we're going."

A squeal of hinges on the opening gate startled Julien, who jumped up and flattened himself against the wall. He hid just out of the pools of lamp light, becoming one of the shadows, if shadows trembled. Seconds later, a horse and carriage clattered out of the courtyard and turned onto the side street before turning again down Dauphine. As it did, Julien could see the pale curve of Zéolie's face in the window lean in and tenderly kiss the man beside her.

Electricity shot through Julien, sizzling and popping in every cell of his body, bringing him to his knees. Bloody, shaking hands flew to his mouth to stifle the scream threatening to burst out as the power in him raged. Hair on his arms and neck stood on end as static gathered in the air surrounding him. It was too much. Too much power to release on the street. It would do too much damage.

This would be far more than shattered glass or a splintered wagon wheel.

Instinctively, Julien threw his hands up and sent the energy skyward. Jagged white lightning streaked across the inky sky, throwing ghastly shadows over the city. Thunder exploded overhead. Windowpanes rattled, and frightened horses reared in their courtyard stalls. Over and over, Julien sent the energy into the night and away from him in an electrical storm until he collapsed, trembling and weak against the wall of the house on Dauphine Street.

Minutes passed that seemed like hours to the tortured mind and soul of Julien Haydel. Fearing the storm, the people of the night sought refuge indoors leaving the streets of the city all but deserted. Only Julien knew where the real danger was. Only he knew it lurked just beneath the surface of what little sanity he had left.

Alone, broken, and exhausted, Julien walked the darkened banquette toward Gallatin Street. He understood now why Zéolie didn't love him. How could she when her heart belonged to another? For a moment, Julien delighted in the thought of removing his competition, but that would only cause Zéolie pain and make her mourn her lost love's memory. No, that would never do. If he was going to have her, she would have to want him instead. And for that, he needed Nora Finnegan.

TWENTY-ONE

The dregs of New Orleans emerged slowly from their hovels on Gallatin Street, only slightly deterred in their deviant pursuits by the electrical storm. Bars bustled with the noise of drunken scum and arguments that spilled into the street. Hustlers lurked in doorways with one eye out for their next mark and the other eye out for the law. In front of one brothel, a dusky-skinned prostitute sat on an overturned bucket with her arms on her knees, hands dangling between her legs. She worked a wad of tobacco in her cheek, spitting amber slime into the gutter. Disgusted, Julien waved a hand at the harlot as he passed, sending the juice down her throat, gagging her. He walked on without stopping, leaving her there coughing and cursing.

Julien slowed his steps as he approached Nora's place, seeing Arthur hovering by her door in the shadows outside of the lamplight. Looking up and seeing Julien, Arthur stiffened, torn between fear and bravado. Not in the mood to deal with trash, Julien leveled a dark, unwavering gaze at him.

"Back again?" Arthur stupidly went with bravado.

"Out of my way," Julien snarled.

Arthur's fear was badly veiled even if Julien hadn't been able to easily tap into his pathetically weak mind. If he had been smarter, Arthur would have swallowed what pride he imagined he had and stepped out of the way. Instead, he planted his feet and met Julien's icy stare, sweat beads shining on his top lip.

The singing voice in his head snarled as Julien's tingling hand flew to Arthur's throat. Digging into the man's windpipe, Julien let the electricity surge from his fingers. Arthur's body jerked violently with the shock before falling limply to the ground.

Julien stepped back and stared down at the corpse at his feet. Horror at what he'd done collided with satisfaction. Bile rose in his throat, and the realization that he'd killed the man settled over him. It was heavy and thick, clinging to his soul. Yet, with it was a rush of power and a release that thrilled him to his core. The snarling voice had begun giggling as the man fell to the ground. Now, she cooed at him as though proud of what he'd done. Straining to hear her words, Julien ached to understand, but it was no use. As she settled back into her song, Julien pushed his guilt down and focused on Arthur.

A stolen glance let Julien know he hadn't been seen, attention having been drawn by a heated argument and hair pulling between two of the whores that were in the brothel doorway up the street. Crouching over the body and running his fingers over the burn marks on Arthur's throat, Julien examined his handiwork. The corpse was still warm to the touch. So close to life, yet so completely in the arms of death. For a moment, Julien indulged his thoughts of the fine line between the living and the dead before pulling his focus back to the task of getting rid of the body.

Moving shards of glass was one thing but moving the dead weight of a body was something he wasn't sure he could do. However, he didn't have time to consider options. The fight down the street was breaking up and customers would be making their way to Nora's house any minute. For the moment, all he could do was get Arthur off the street and into the narrow space where the lop-sided angle of the brothel met the building next door. It would have to do until he could deal with it after the nightcrawlers went to their beds to sleep off the evening's debauchery.

Directing energy through both hands, he slid Arthur's corpse into the dark narrow space, just deep enough to be out of sight of anyone passing by. Later, he'd dump the body in the river. But first, he needed to see Nora.

"Wasn't sure you'd show up, Paris," Nora said with her crimson grin as she opened the door for him. She leaned on the doorframe, leaving only enough space for him to pass that he'd have to brush against her to get inside. "Figured you'd decide you're too good for us."

"I am," Julien said curtly, "but it doesn't mean I don't have a use for you." The air inside the room was close and thick. His head was swimming and the stifling stillness wasn't helping.

"Well, bein' useful is somethin' we know all about here. Long as you pay for it," Nora returned. Consummate businesswoman.

Julien's eyes scanned the room and found it much the same way it had been the previous night. Girls entertaining guests of questionable repute draped themselves across laps while their customers bought drinks. Nora, madam and bartender, took their money, but cut the drinks for her girls with water. Smart, Julien thought. The girls stay sober while the dates get drunk enough to be fleeced, and less alcohol poured means more profit. While she was at the bar, she fixed two glasses of whiskey and handed one to Julien. Then, she led him to a corner of the room with two soft chairs.

Julien reached into his pocket to pay for the drink, but she held out a hand to stop him. "Put your money away. We'll take care of that later," she said, settling in the chair next to him. "Now, that handsome face of yours is darker'n it was last night. Tell Nora what happened."

Whiskey burned its way down his throat and warmed the blood that was ice cold after killing Arthur. Julien toyed with the idea of telling Nora what he had done but decided it could wait. Instead, he just shook his head.

"C'mon, Paris, you can't fool me. Spill it," the madam coaxed.

Julien rested the glass on his knee and ran a hand through his dark hair. His head ached as the adrenaline of the early evening left his veins. "I went to see her."

Nora leaned back in the chair and twisted a strand of hair around her finger, a habit that was becoming familiar. In that moment, Julien's heart ached for the afternoons spent in Zéolie's parlor with the Marchon girls. What he wouldn't give to be back there trying not to let his eyes settle on Celeste's long legs crossed across from him, watching her wind a long strand of her hair around a young graceful finger. She wanted him, even if Zéolie didn't. And he wouldn't have to pay for her affection.

"And she didn't want to see you," Nora said, bringing him back to his sordid reality.

"Something like that," he grumbled. "She didn't even know I was there. I overheard her in the courtyard talking. Her voice was easy to pick out, but I didn't know the others. It wasn't her usual group of friends. A Haitian Creole, and..." His words left him as the image of Zéolie kissing the young man in the carriage consumed him.

"And a man. But not just any man, I see." Nora tapped a long nail on the side of her glass. "Looks like that plan of yours is gonna take a bit more doin' that we thought if you want to get rid of 'im."

"No," Julien said sharply. "Same plan. I can't take him from her and expect her to love me. She has to want me more."

Nora nodded. "Alright, then." Sharp eyes under heavily colored lids scanned the room. "Where do you want to start? I've got a couple girls who are givin' me hell lately. Want one of them?"

"We'll work up to that. I need to know what I can do with someone less headstrong and more...pliable," Julien said. "And don't give me any of your money makers just yet. They may fall madly in love with me, or they may drop dead. Who knows?"

"You're my money maker, now, Paris. Take whoever you want."

He realized Nora chose the spot in the corner of the room on purpose. From his vantage point he could watch the girls come and go. Flirting, talking, and arguing with each other. All of them were crass and missing teeth. One was missing an eye under a black patch that he was certain she'd stolen from a pirate. Each of them was an open book to him.

Two of the girls were arguing over one of the men and whose turn it was. The argument quickly escalated to the point where it was going to come to blows. Couples strewn around the parlor watched and giggled.

"God damn it," Nora swore as she got up to put an end to the bickering. Julien silently removed the two quarrelsome whores from the list of prospects for his first experiment.

Before the parlor traffic began to slow and the last of the customers staggered out, Julien settled on who he would ask Nora for. She was a scrawny brunette with short curls around her face and a long braid down her back. Watching her through the night, Julien learned she was new to the city from up river and without family to help her.

Or miss her, Julien thought. Once he'd made his choice, Julien signaled to Nora, who began loading the girl's drinks. She added to the other harlots' drinks, too, just to make sure they slept hard enough to not be easily awakened by whatever happened with Julien. By the time the last of the men were shown out, the chosen girl was a staggering drunk.

"Gisèle," Nora called to her as the girls were headed upstairs. "Paris here wants to see you."

The girl rocked onto the balls of her feet, swaying with the alcohol, then turned around with a flirtatious grin. "Oh, he does, does he?" she asked, running a finger along the plunging neckline of her top.

"Easy, Gisèle," Nora scolded. "Not like that."

Gisèle's face fell. "Fine, but he doesn't know what he's missin'."

"I'll take your word for it," Julien answered. "I have a different kind of job for you."

The girl's interest was piqued, but she wasn't drunk enough to be completely off-guard. "What kind of job? What do you want me to do?"

Julien winked at her. "Just stand there and look pretty," he said, taking Gisèle by the arm and leading her to Nora's bedroom in the back of the house.

Nora bolted the front door and grabbed the bottle of whiskey as she followed them back. "Somethin' tells me we're gonna need this."

DRUNK AND PLIABLE, Gisèle stood on one side of Nora's bedroom, swaying like she was on a small boat on a rough sea. Julien's skin crawled from where the girl hung on him trying to tempt him into letting her do her job while he fed her enough whiskey to put a sailor under the table. Barely upright, the girl leaned back against the faded wallpaper and closed her eyes.

"Not yet, Gisèle," Julien said. "I need you awake for this."

"For what?" she asked, her head lolling to one side as she squinted at him.

"Lookin' pretty." Nora laughed. "You ready?" she asked Julien.

Julien shrugged. His stomach churned and the voice in the back of his mind changed from singing to laughing again. A low rumbling chuckle.

"I guess I'll have to be. We don't have much time before she's out." Nora nodded reassuringly, but Julien was anything but ready to try this. Yet, he didn't have it in him to back out now. He couldn't let Nora see his weakness. Her silence depended as much on the money he was paying her as it did her own fear of what he was capable of. Whether he was confident in his strength or not, he had to make a show of it.

Nora moved behind him, out of the way of whatever was going to be heading for Gisèle as Julien focused on what he wanted from the girl. She stood there, dirty and half-dressed, reeking of alcohol and cigarettes, so unlike the woman he wanted so desperately. Gisèle disgusted him, but it wasn't really her affection he was after anyway. He just needed to know he could command it. Without price.

Focusing on Zéolie, he let the electricity course through him. Trying not to think about the broken pieces of his heart, he brought her face to the front of his mind. The face he loved. Warm, familiar, and stunning. So different from the creature leaning against the flimsy wall across the room. Heat settled in his fingertips as his heart ached for Zéolie again. He loved her, no matter how angry he was at her for tossing that love away. Julien wanted her more than anything and would stop at nothing to have her want him, too.

The pounding of his heart in his ears returned as blood coursed through his veins, mingling with the electricity. Beneath the drumming of his heart was the low laugh. Not mocking now. Expectant. Coaxing him on. Whispering words he couldn't understand.

Julien's fingers flexed at his side nervously as he kept Zéolie's face in his mind. Laughing and flirting over the balcony. It may not have meant anything to her, but it was genuine no matter how much she wanted to deny it. Taking a slow, measured breath to steel himself against the current racing along his veins, he raised both hands out in front of him and held them there. Another breath, and Zéolie's face was laughing at him again as the burst of energy slammed into Gisèle, shattering her collar bone. The girl shrieked. Julien panicked and another burst sent her through the wall into the next room. A scream threatened to fly from Nora's mouth, but she slapped her hand over it to choke it back, terrified Julien would take aim at her next.

Cracked plaster and torn pink brocade wallpaper hung in tatters around the jagged opening. Dust swirled in the lamplight like a fog. Vomit threatened to rise in his throat as Julien stepped through the hole in the wall and saw the mangled body lying motionless in a growing pool of red on the shabby rug.

"Get rid of it," he ordered. With a wave of his hand, he rolled the rug around the corpse and walked back through the hole in the wall.

"The girls would've heard that. It's a damn good thing they're drunk and stupid or I'd never be able to explain this mess." Nora looked at the crumbling plaster, then at Julien. "Maybe we need to find somewhere less fragile."

Julien wasn't sure how he felt about the fact that Nora seemed to be more concerned about the damage to her house than the dead girl on the floor. "I'll pay for it," he said.

"Never doubted that. I just don't want the place to cave in on us if you don't get this right on the next try."

Julien sat heavily on the edge of Nora's bed, sinking into the well-worn mattress and running his hands through his dark hair.

"You know," Nora said quietly, "this ain't really somethin' I've got much experience in—"

Julien glared at her.

"Alright. No experience. I've got no experience in this kind of thing, but I'm thinkin' you don't either," Nora said cautiously. "How are you expectin' to learn how to do any of this if you don't have any control?"

He sighed. "I'll figure it out. I just need more practice."

Nora walked over to the hole in the wall. "Then I guess I won't go fixin' this just yet." As she left him alone, she said over her shoulder, "But if it were me, I'd work on gettin' my head on straight before I mess with power I can't control. Wouldn't want it backfirin'."

Exhausted and aggravated, Julien threw a candlestick at the door as it shut behind her.

TWENTY-TWO

Zéolie hesitated as she stepped over the threshold of the convent parlor. Memories flooded over her of the last time she sat in this room with the Marchons. The rawness of her father's death, the mania of her mother haunting her mind, and the fear of the unknown. It was the unknown that was often the most frightening. How does someone brace for danger they can't see coming? What terrors lurk in the darkness of the mind when it's fractured with hatred and madness? Even now, she shuddered at the thought of that madness infecting Julien. Infecting her brother. Steeling herself for the news she dreaded hearing, Zéolie settled into the chair by the window to watch for the arrival of the Marchons' carriage.

"Not here yet?" Louis asked, scanning the room as he walked in.

Zéolie sighed. "Not yet." Louis bent down and kissed her cheek before taking the seat across from her. "*Chérie,*" she said, "do you think it's a good idea to have them just walk in and see you here? They don't even know you're alive. Shouldn't we tell them first and let it sink in slowly?"

Louis grinned. "Maybe you're right. I'd hate to put the girls through more shock, even if it's a good one." With a squeeze of her hand, he stood to go. "I'll have Squire just outside. Send him to get me when you're ready."

Zéolie nodded and Louis kissed the corner of her mouth before slipping quietly out of the parlor. Impatient, she resumed her pacing until wheels crunched in the front drive. Pulling the edge of the curtain aside, she saw the stately Marchon carriage.

Moments later, Squire was outside, holding the door open for the women and helping them down. Mother Micheaux stood a few paces away with her hands clasped at her waist, appearing pious and strong despite the war raging around and inside her. Since her return from the Haydel plantation and her confrontation with Jean-Jacques, the mother superior had been pale and tired. Something told Zéolie that more than a conversation happened that day, and whatever it was took a toll on the nun, physically and spiritually. Letting the curtain close gently back into place, Zéolie took a deep breath as she once more prepared to get the Marchon women filled in on the chaos of her own life that directly affected theirs.

Madame Marchon swept into the room as Zéolie rose to meet her. "*Chérie*, it's so good to see you," the matron said, taking Zéolie's hands in hers. "We've been worried about you since that business at the party."

"I'm sorry I left you to deal with the guests and the mess."

"Nonsense, child. You knew where you needed to be and I'm perfectly able to handle a social episode," Madame Marchon said with a dismissive wave of her hand.

Celeste sat in a chair near the door and said, "You should have seen her, Zéolie! In minutes, she had all of the dish fragments scooped up in the tablecloth and turned the whole party into a picnic around the fountain."

"How did you explain the explosion of glass and china?" Zéolie asked.

Madame Marchon smiled. "Lovers quarrel. No one was completely sure what they saw because it couldn't really have happened the way they thought, so it was easy enough to simply say nothing and let them wonder."

Lisette sat next to Celeste as Madame Marchon, Zéolie, and Mother Micheaux took their seats around the room. "That lovers quarrel thing, Zéolie. What happened?"

"Really, Zéolie," Celeste chimed in, "how could you upset Julien like that? He's perfect!"

Zéolie sighed and folded her hands. With a nod from her, Squire left his post and headed down the hall. "There's something you need to know." Glancing at the mother superior, who nodded, she went on. "I had a good reason at the time, and now I have one more."

"What reason could you possibly've had to make him storm out like that?" Celeste said indignantly. "It was pretty clear how he feels about you. If only I could get him to look at me the way he looks at you!"

"Celeste," snapped Madame Marchon. "Go on, Zéolie."

Heat rose in her cheeks as she thought about how Julien poured his heart out to her hoping she felt the same way. It was bashful and sweet. Genuine. "He told me that he didn't intend to, but he'd fallen in love with me."

A little squeak escaped from Listette, the romantic.

"I had to tell him I didn't feel the same way. I told him I was grateful to have him as a friend, but that's all I could and wanted to ever be."

"But *why?*" Lisette asked, unable to control herself anymore.

Zéolie sighed. "I couldn't bring myself to tell him that night, but my heart belongs to Louis." The laugh echoing in her mind seemed to change as she said it. From haunting and distant, to menacing and close. Too close. Chills trickled down her arms, making her pull them in tight.

Celeste's incredulous expression softened. "Zéolie, I know you miss him and love him, but he wouldn't want you to be lonely on his account. Louis'd want you to find someone who would love you like he can't anymore."

Lisette chimed in, "I hate to say it, but Celeste's right."

"I'm not sure Louis would agree with you," Mother Micheaux said. Her voice startled the Marchon girls, who had completely forgotten she was there.

"What do you mean?" Madame Marchon asked.

"Zéolie?" the nun asked.

Nodding, Zéolie answered, "Because Louis is…" How were they going to take another resurrected friend? She had no choice but to just spit it out. "…alive."

Madame Marchon's hand went to her heart, and all of the women's eyes stared at their friend. Clearly shaken, Madame Marchon asked, "How? I don't understand."

Mother Micheaux stepped in to explain. "While I was taking care of Zéolie here, Nell was caring for Louis. After a while, she'd done all she could and was concerned that he wasn't going to pull through. It was then that she brought him to me." She paused and looked at Zéolie. "To us. By then, Zéolie was strong enough to help us bring him back."

"I don't believe this," Celeste whispered. She rose and paced circles around her chair as she tried to process what she heard. Lisette sat dumbly in her chair, staring at the wall.

Madame Marchon's eyes narrowed looking from Zéolie to the mother superior. "You mean you brought *both of them* back?"

"Not alone," the nun clarified.

"Wait—" Celeste began. "I thought Mama Nell brought her back? It was *you*?"

"But you're a—a—" Lisette stammered as words began to come back to her. "—a *nun!*"

Madame Marchon, who seemed completely unsurprised by the news of the nun's dark abilities, pulled the conversation back to the point. "Girls, that's enough." Then softly to Mother Micheaux, "How is he?"

A wan smile flickered across the nun's face as she looked past Madame Marchon. "See for yourself," she said with a nod to the parlor doorway.

All three of the Marchon women turned to see Louis Soucier standing framed in the threshold smiling sheepishly at them with his hands in his pockets. In the pregnant silence that followed, he became more uncomfortable under their stares and drew a hand out to push a curl from his forehead. Cutting his eyes at Zéolie, he shrugged as the women stared.

"Ladies," he said at last, "it's good to see you again."

Lisette fainted in her chair and Celeste plopped down heavily in hers.

"So much for easing the shock," he said weakly. Zéolie rushed over to fan Lisette and get the girl sitting up again.

Only Madame Marchon was able to find words, weak though they were. "Good to see you, too, Louis." She held out her hand to him, giving him the confidence he needed to come into the room.

Kissing her hand, he then turned to the girls. "Are they going to be alright? We were hoping to lessen the shock by letting Zéolie tell them first."

"They'll be fine," Madame Marchon said. "Celeste, close your mouth." The girl did, but her eyes never left Louis.

Zéolie knelt at Lisette's side, patting her hand. "I guess you can see now why it was so easy for me to refuse Julien."

"Quite," Madame Marchon said with a smile. "But you said you had two reasons. Has something else happened?"

"You mean besides the fact that Julien could obliterate an entire dinner setting with a wave of his hand?" Louis asked.

"I admit, I've had some questions about that, but assumed Zéolie would tell me when she had answers," the matron said, settling back into her seat.

Mother Micheaux stood and paced the room for a moment before she spoke. Her hands trembled and keeping them folded at her waist was the only way for her to hide the turmoil she felt. Under her wimple, sweat gathered cold and damp on her forehead. Droplets gathered between her shoulder blades and slid down the middle of her back. She was the leader of the Ursuline nuns and had to once more admit herself as a woman who ordered the death of a child. It didn't matter if her order was ignored. She gave it and that was enough to torment her. Enough to condemn her.

The mother superior sighed and began, "As you gathered, there's more to Julien Haydel than we first thought. What he was able to do is because of who he is." She paused and looked at the three innocent women staring expectantly at her.

Zéolie felt Mother Micheaux's agony at having to thrust the Marchon family once more into danger. It just wasn't fair that her family should once more be the cause of their fear.

The nun closed her eyes for a moment, gray lashes fluttering uncertainly on wrinkled cheeks, opened them again and began. "Julien's arrival in New Orleans as the young man you know wasn't the first time I met him. When I saw him for the first time, he was a baby in the arms of his mother."

Lisette perked up a little. "So, you know the woman he's looking for?"

"Knew. I *knew* the woman he's looking for."

"What do you mean?" Madame Marchon asked.

"Julien's mother is dead. At least, as far as I know."

Lisette's innocent face fell. "That's terrible. I was hoping he'd find her."

"Not likely," Zéolie said. "Turns out, we all knew his mother in some way." With a pained look at Louis, she added, "Some of us more than others." Louis shifted uncomfortably in his seat but said nothing.

Celeste leaned forward. "How? Who is she—*was* she?"

Mother Micheaux lowered her eyes, tears welling up in them.

"Julien is the child of the nephew of Jean-Jacques Haydel and Solène Marie Cheval."

Shock and disbelief crashed over the women in a tidal wave of emotion. Words spoken so softly seemed to reverberate against the convent walls, shaking it to its foundation. Zéolie knew what it felt like to hear those words and let them sink in slowly, knowing their barbs would catch and sting before finally settling in their minds. Eyes of the women darted from Zéolie, to Louis, to Mother Micheaux, frantically searching for there to be some mistake, but there was none to be found.

Again, it was Madame Marchon that found her words first. A whisper of disbelief. "It can't be true."

"I'm afraid so," Mother Micheaux answered. Memories of the past hid in the dark corners of her mind, hiding from the light. Cowering there. Trembling as they were dragged out of her mouth. "Solène escaped after she tried to kill Zéolie as a baby. She found her way to the outskirts of the Haydel property and made camp. Before long, Jean-Jacques' nephew found her and they had Julien, of course named for the one man she truly loved. We managed to capture her again and take the baby from her, but the Haydels wanted nothing to do with the child of a witch. We were afraid of what she'd do if she got him back, so -" Pain contorted her face as she spoke her sin. "- I ordered Jean-Jacques to—to kill the boy."

"My god," Madame Marchon whispered. A delicate gloved hand clutched at her chest as she stared at the dark nun.

Tears streamed down Mother Micheaux's cheeks, hot and relentless as she fought to keep control of her emotions. Ignoring their splashing on her robes, she fought through her full confession, "It was wrong, I know. Panic makes us foolish, and fear blinds us, but it made sense then."

Lisette turned wide, stunned eyes on the mother superior and asked, "But he's alive. What happened?"

"Jean-Jacques couldn't bring himself to do it, so he hid the boy instead."

"And apparently his mother," Louis added.

Madame Marchon's brows knit. "Haydel hid *Solène*?"

Zéolie nodded. "She managed to escape a second time, made it back to the plantation camp, and Jean-Jacques hid her and the child. Likely out of fear of Solène's wrath. Eventually, they sent Julien to France."

"What did Solène do after that?" Madame Marchon asked.

Louis shrugged. "That, we don't know." He glanced at Mother Micheaux before asking, "Do we?"

The mother superior hung her head, knowing it was a pointed question from the former police officer who knew her propensity for withholding the truth. "No," she answered softly and honestly.

Madame Marchon rose from her chair and tucked a graying auburn lock behind her ear as she paced the floor in thought. "If Julien is Solène's son, he's inherited her abilities. So, it's not just the women."

"Apparently not," Zéolie answered.

"And the madness?" the matron asked.

"We don't know," Mother Micheaux said.

Zéolie added, "Before his outburst at the party, there was nothing that made any of us concerned about his sanity. It could've been a moment of anger, or it could've been the beginnings of madness. Until we see him again, we won't know."

Lisette's face was white as she spoke. "If he can do what your mother could do—what *you* can do—and he's angry..." Color drained from her lips, the bottom one wavering as she fought back tears and fear.

"He's dangerous even without the madness if he's angry and hurt," Louis finished. "Which is why we asked you to come here. You needed to know that you're in very real danger.

Celeste had been deathly quiet as the others talked, but finally spoke. Her words were soft and strained, as she pushed herself out of her chair, swaying slightly. "Julien wouldn't do that. He couldn't. He's not like her. Not like that—that maniac." Her eyes were filled with tears as her voice trailed off. Zéolie realized in that moment how much of Celeste's flirtations were actually a cover for her real emotions. Feelings she was willing to swallow for her friend's happiness before she knew any of this. Celeste Marchon was in love with Julien Haydel.

CHAPTER

TWENTY-THREE

Afternoon sun streaked through the filthy wavy glass as it sank below the rooftops. Julien woke in Nora's whorehouse drenched in sweat. Electricity pulsed through his body. Emotions quarreled with one another as he tried to sort out the dreams from reality. The line between the two was becoming more blurred as his sleep was filled with growing nightmares that seemed increasingly real. Places he didn't recognize and the woman whose voice rang in his head. A cabin in the middle of the deep black swamp, and a ramshackle hut in the clearing of earthy woods. Always, she was there like she was when he was awake. Laughing, singing, but always garbled. Only once had the woman spoken to him clearly even though he begged her to do it again.

She was there again last night, laughing and cackling on top of the roof of a cabin he didn't know but had seen in his dreams before. Her features were hazy as he stood at the edge of the flaming swamp, heat rising from the flames blurring her face, but he knew it was her voice. Crossing the line between unconsciousness and consciousness, he could have sworn there was someone else there with him. Someone he never saw, watching him from the shadows. He could feel their presence, but before he had a chance to discover who it was, the dream ended in a blinding white flash.

Rubbing sleep and uncertainty from his eyes, Julien saw the results of the previous night's experiment sitting placidly in a chair in the corner, staring blankly ahead. Compliant, but without any mind of her own.

After the disaster of the first girl, he gained some control over the direction and intensity of the energy he thrust at them, but it always ended the same way. Tortured and bloodied, the girls lay dead on the floor. He could destroy, but he couldn't command. Now, sitting in the chair staring at him, or rather through him, was the last of the experiments. Alive, but vacant. Worthless. Julien wanted to compel Zéolie's passion and love, not make her a mindless idiot.

"Do you love me?" he asked the girl curled up in the chair. Nothing. No answer. No change in expression. Blankness. Failure seized him, and anger roared in his mind. With a jerk of his head, the girl's neck snapped where she sat, and she fell limply draped over the back of the chair.

Exasperated, Julien got up, dressed, and strode out into the Quarter. The black look on his face as he stormed out of the brothel was enough to let Nora know she had one less girl working tonight.

The voice in his head was relentless in her wordless singing and laughing, depending on what Julien was doing. Her laugh grew wicked and sharp as he experimented on Nora's girls, but lulled him with singing in his frustration and failure. "You're no help, you know," Julien snapped at the voice. She stopped singing and chuckled, then went back to her song as he pushed past rabble on Gallatin Street toward anywhere but there.

His brilliant plan to command Zéolie's affection had fallen as flat as the corpses left in his wake. With no direction or outlet, the pent-up energy pulsed through him, threatening to unleash on any passerby. If he didn't get control of this, something was going to happen that would draw more attention than some shattered china and a handful of dead prostitutes.

Inside Julien's fractured mind, thoughts of his mother pushed back to the surface. He'd foolishly let Zéolie take him away from his search. All the time wasted on her could have been better spent finding his missing mother. Guilt at allowing his heart to run away with his mind consumed him on top of the fury and frustration. A whirlpool of emotions pulled at the pit of his stomach that churned with nausea. Cold sweat broke out on his brow, and his hands trembled uncontrollably. Vomit burned his throat as it forced its way up.

Emptying the contents of his stomach in the alley behind the row of brothels and bars, he braced himself on a wall as the world spun for a moment before coming back into focus. "I have to get out of here." It didn't matter where, it just needed to be soon.

With the money he had left after buying off Nora and her girls, Julien made his way to the riverfront warehouses. Lined up alongside the market was an endless row of carts and saddled horses shifting their weight on the uneven bricks. Scanning the crowd for someone looking to make a deal, Julien saw a man lingering by his horse at the end of the row. Dirty clothes, greasy hair, and a wadded hat in his hands marked him as a man who needed some cash. Within minutes Julien was in the saddle and the man was hurrying into the market amazed at his good fortune and the decisiveness of the well-dressed Frenchman.

At first the horse was skittish with her new rider, but Julien's firm hand quickly brought her under control as he rode out of the Quarter. Never having been outside the city since his arrival, he had no idea where he was headed and didn't care. The ride felt good and gave him something to focus on as he learned the quirks of the black horse under him.

Energy coursing through his veins evened out as he rode further away from the city and Zéolie. In the quiet of the river road, the singing voice seemed more present than ever. Not simply existing in the depths of his thoughts, but almost riding alongside him, as if he could reach out and touch her. The words were almost clear in her familiar song, but not quite. It was as though he was underwater listening to a voice on the surface. The melody was clear, but the words themselves were garbled. Only once in a while would a word or two come through, but not enough for him to place the song.

Wind from the river churning next to him ran its fingers through his hair. The cooler air helped to calm the nausea that had settled on him in the Quarter earlier. Fresh air brought clarity to his thoughts that were mired in his passion for controlling Zéolie. While the urge to bend her to his will hadn't changed, his desire for her wavered. More time spent with Nora and her habits of crossing her legs and twirling long strands of hair brought Celeste Marchon to mind almost as much as Zéolie. Celeste wanted him. That much he knew. If her flirtations had been lost on him, her thoughts weren't.

Julien's mind wandered to thoughts he'd not paid much attention to in his focus on Zéolie. Celeste was open about her feelings for him and yet he'd pushed those thoughts aside before. Most were embarrassingly forward, but others were more genuine. There was a sweetness in her thoughts that was shielded by her sarcasm and wit on the outside. A vulnerability she refused to expose. Had his heart not been eclipsed by the mysterious pull of Zéolie, he could easily have found himself falling for Celeste.

Julien wasn't able to entertain these thoughts for long as the voice in his head became agitated. Her sing-song became a darker, almost snarling, laugh the longer he focused on Celeste. Pulling his thoughts back to Zéolie and the search for his mother seemed to appease the voice, bringing it back to a lighter laugh and sporadic singing. Until he knew what that voice was, Julien thought better of making her angry, especially as close as she seemed at the moment.

She settled back into her wordless song and Julien's thoughts drifted again. His mind darted to Zéolie and the failed attempts of controlling the girls at Nora's. Bloody mindless messes that they were. His stomach knotted at the thought that he could have done that to Zéolie if he hadn't practiced first. Amused by the idea, the voice chuckled merrily as Julien's stomach threatened to reject the little food he'd put in it.

With each mile put between him and the city, the more fractured his thoughts became. Freedom and clarity were slowly clouded by compulsion and chaos. Thoughts jumped madly from Zéolie to his mother, then to Celeste. With each flashing thought came a different outburst from the voice. Wickedly amused at Zéolie, syrupy sweet towards his mother, and menacing with Celeste. He could no more control the thoughts and emotions surging through his mind than he could the energy in his veins. Desperately, he tried to sort them out and quiet the noise, but only grew more frustrated with the effort. Even the horse seemed to sense the turmoil and became nervous and twitchy.

Hours passed as the voice constantly made her opinions about Julien's thoughts known through her laughter and song. More and more, he was pulled back to his need to control Zéolie, but for a reason he was struggling to remember. No longer did it seem like a conscious decision, but a compulsion. Riding on, with no direction at all, his mood darkened along with the sky as he struggled to take control of thoughts that wandered to cabins, swamps, and pretty faces. Electricity pulsed through his veins as he continued the journey along the river road, pulled by blind instinct toward something. Julien had no idea where but knew without a doubt it was where he was supposed to be.

CHAPTER

TWENTY-FOUR

Darkness spread its arms wide in the deep swamp, embracing every living thing. Overhead, a sliver of moon shone down, dripping diamonds on the black water. Sounds of night creatures filled the shadows with their eerie song. Silently moving through whispering reeds, fearsome beasts hunted in the depths of the trees. Water diamonds scattered in ripples as a leathery reptile slid its massive body under the inky surface.

Zéolie stood transfixed by it all at the foot of Mama Nell's cabin. As encompassing as the sensations were, she knew she wasn't really there. Dreams were becoming more vivid since Julien's birthday party, and this was one more of them. Knowing that didn't make them any less frightening. Anything can happen in dreams, and if the dream is walking the line of reality, she didn't know what very real perils it might hold for her.

Wind moved the grasses at her feet and swirled upwards through the cypress canopy above. Her hand went out to one of the stilts that held the cabin aloft to steady herself. The aging wood was damp with humidity and soft with lichen that grew in the cracks. A low whistle wound its way around the corner of the house as the wind danced past, lifting a strand of her hair and settling it gently on her shoulder.

Her body tingled, every cell on edge, standing in this familiar place that had changed somehow. Dark eyes searched for differences that were difficult to spot. A new roof that had already lost its shine and begun to age in the wet swamp air and Louisiana heat. Wide vertical planks that formed the cabin walls were variegated in color next to others with soot-stained tops, revealing the new ones placed there after a fire.

Fire. Zéolie's mind threatened to sink into Louis' memories of the night in the swamp when the cabin ignited along with her mother, but she forced those thoughts back, fearing what would happen here if she let them come. No, she was in this place for another reason. There was something she needed to see. She knew that as clearly as she knew it was a dream and searched for a sign of what that reason could be.

Time passed slowly in the swamp with only the night creatures' sounds and movements to let her know it passed at all. *Maybe I was wrong. Maybe there's nothing for me here.*

As the thought faded, so did the serenity of the swamp. Flames roared into existence in a ring surrounding her. *No!* she panicked. *Not again!* There was no heat to the fire as it shimmered. No substance. Relaxing some in the knowledge that the flames couldn't hurt her, she slipped into the shadows under the stilts to watch the scene play out. Hollow laughter filled the emptiness, echoing over the popping and hissing of the flames. She knew that voice too well. Solène.

Sparks rained down from the roof as Zéolie backed further out of sight. Dream or not, she wasn't taking any chances. Her mother's cackling laughter concentrated above her near the roof as a transparent figure appeared at the edge of the tree line. For a moment, Zéolie thought she was in Louis' memories again, but this figure was different. Taller. Darker. Slowly, the shape solidified. "Julien!" she gasped.

Panic seized her thoughts. If Julien was watching this, he was connected somehow to Solène. There was no other explanation for it. And if he was connected to her to the point where she controlled his dreams, Solène could manipulate him. What else had she shown him? Solène had brought Julien here, but who brought her? Until this moment, Zéolie thought Camille wanted her in the dream swamp to give her some sort of message, but now she wasn't sure. Could her mother have brought her back here like Julien?

"No," Zéolie hissed. "This stops now." Zéolie held her arms straight down at her side with her palms outward, gathering the energy around her. Her fingertips tingled, then began to burn with the building power. Holding her palms in front of her, she pushed the growing energy into a shield of blinding white. With the fading light, the images around her disintegrated into blackness. As they did, Zéolie sat bolt upright on the cot in the chamber under the convent, surrounded once more by the familiar earthiness.

Louis was instantly by her side. "What happened?" he asked, taking her hand in his as he wiped beads of sweat from her forehead. Blue veins streaked across her strained face.

"The cabin," Zéolie said, trying to calm her breathing. "It was different this time."

"What do you mean?" Mama Nell asked, sitting on the foot of the bed.

"I could see the cabin, but it wasn't like my own memories. The roof had been replaced, and parts of the walls. Some places were blackened—"

"—by fire," Mama Nell finished. Her mossy eyes met the dark ones of her niece. "*Chérie*, that wasn't your memory. After the fire, the cabin was rebuilt while I was tendin' to Louis. New roof and wallboards. Some of 'em were salvageable but darkened by the fire. What you saw in your dream was the cabin as it stands now."

"But how?" asked Louis. "She hasn't been back there."

Mama Nell nodded. "I know. There's no reason for her to know that unless someone wanted 'er to see it. To be there."

Louis thought for a moment. "Camille?"

Zéolie shook her head. "I don't think so. The house wasn't the only difference. There was someone else there watching Solène on the roof. At first, I thought it was you, from your memory, until the figure became clearer."

"Did you know 'em?" Mama Nell asked.

"It was Julien."

Color drained from Nell's face as it dawned on her what that could mean. "My god," she whispered. "That means…"

Zéolie nodded but Louis stayed confused. "I don't understand," he said, looking from one woman to the other who seemed to know perfectly well what that meant.

"Solène's got control of her son," Mama Nell said bluntly. "Can't nothin' good come of that." The priestess stood and straightened her flowing skirt and scarves. "Louis, go see if you can find Mother Micheaux. Me an' Zéolie'll get things ready down here."

"Ready for what?" Louis asked as he went to the door.

"To build a bridge. Camille's Julien's grandmother, too. Maybe she can show us what's goin' on."

Louis nodded and went to find the mother superior.

"Do you think this'll work?" Zéolie asked as Louis closed the door behind him.

Mama Nell shrugged. "Gettin' Camille to help'll be a damn sight easier'n it was last time since we dealt with the guilt holdin' her back. Whether or not she can show us what's goin' on in that boy's mind, well, that's another thing. But," she said flatly, "it's the only thing we got." The priestess touched her niece's cheek and added, "First, though, tea."

Louis found the mother superior in her office alone. As much as all of this was wearing on her, she still looked commanding behind her desk. "Mother?" he asked gently, trying not to let his own panic startle her.

She wasn't an easy one to fool. "What's happened?" she asked pointedly.

"Zéolie's dream. She was back at the cabin, but not in her own memory. She could see it after the repairs. And she wasn't alone."

Mother Micheaux rose slowly. "Julien?" she asked.

Louis nodded. "How'd you know?"

"It's the only person that makes sense." She slammed a hand on her desk. "*Damn it!* There's only one way the boy would be able to see that cabin." Her already pale face whitened under her wimple. Beads of sweat broke out on her thin upper lip as she fought to hide the frustration and fear building in her.

"Nell asked me to come get you. She says they're going to build a bridge with Camille, hoping she can give some answers to what's happening with Julien and Solène."

Mother Micheaux nodded as she led him quickly back down the corridor. "It's worth a try. What's happening isn't hard to figure out. It's how she's doing it and how much control she has over him. And what she's planning to do with that control."

"Could she be trying to use him like she wanted to use Zéolie?" Louis asked.

"Possibly. Who knows with that woman? Solène could be using him to get to his sister. And after Zéolie rejected his affections, Julien could be only too willing to let her. We just have to hope Zéolie's stronger than her brother."

"She's had control over what she can do long enough. Surely, she can outmatch him."

Mother Micheaux shook her head. "That's not what I'm worried about but make no mistake. Out of control magic can be just as dangerous as focused power. Zéolie knows that only too well. No, I'm hoping she's strong enough to do what she has to do if it comes down to a fight between the two of them." Passing Squire in the hall, she nodded at him and the boy followed on their heels.

～

ONCE MORE LOUIS stood on the outside of a ring of salt as the anchor to reality should anything go wrong with the women's efforts to contact Camille. As the drum went silent under Squire's hands, the three women slipped seamlessly into their trances, smoke hanging thickly around them in the candlelight. Energy hummed in the air, pulsing as they passed it through their joined hands. The eyes of all three women rolled back, only needing to see what was in their minds.

"Camille?" Zéolie asked softly. Her voice echoed in the space surrounding her.

"I'm here," came the answer.

Silver mist gathered in the emptiness in front of Zéolie, becoming more solid. For a moment, the memory of Camille pushing Zéolie's spirit back into her body flooded her as she watched the form of her grandmother take shape. Then Camille's figure transformed from mist to the rippled form of their first encounter. She seemed to float just out of Zéolie's reach, long silvery hair rising and falling as though she was underwater being carried by a gentle current. Her long, loose gown flowed on the ripples and shimmered at edges that didn't quite come into focus. Without the guilt holding her back, Camille's connection to her granddaughter was stronger than ever.

Zéolie smiled. "Good to see you again."

"You, too," Camille answered, returning the smile. "I know you didn't go through all of this just to see an old woman."

Not knowing how much time she had with the apparition, Zéolie got straight to the point. "I need your help."

Camille's smile faded. "Julien?"

Zéolie nodded. "And Solène."

Her grandmother's face darkened. "Solène doesn't let me in like you do. I can't see her thoughts to know what she's done," she said, shaking her head, silvery hair swirling. "She's blocking me."

"Thoughts? Is she—is she *alive*?" Zéolie asked, dumbstruck.

Camille knit her brow in thought. "Something like her should burn in hell if she was dead," she spat, "but she walks in the shadows between life and death. Solène's rage and madness when she died chained her to the living. There was no peaceful release for her spirit."

"Between the living and the dead," Zéolie repeated. "That's how she's controlling Julien."

Camille's eyes locked with Zéolie's. "What?"

For some reason, Zéolie assumed being dead would open levels of knowledge for her grandmother. Omniscience of sorts. Then again, she did have to explain to Camille that she wasn't responsible for all of the mess they were in. Once more, she set about to give her grandmother answers so she could get a few of her own. "Since Julien revealed himself for what he is, my dreams've become vivid. Most are memories, but the last one was different. Something I couldn't have known on my own. I thought it was you who brought me to the cabin in the swamp."

"No, *chérie*," Camille said. "I'd never trespass in your dreams. I get your attention when I need to in other ways."

Like almost knocking me out of a chair, Zéolie thought.

"Exactly," Camille said, hearing the thought as clearly as if Zéolie said it out loud.

"Someone wanted me to see the cabin, and I wasn't alone there," Zéolie explained. "As I watched the fire ignite the trees and encircle the house, Julien was in the tree line watching the same scene."

"I don't understand. Why would she want him to see that?" Camille asked. "And why would she want you to see it, too?"

"I was hoping you'd know."

Camille slowly shook her head. "I wish I did."

Zéolie tried one last thing to get the answers she needed. "Can you see Julien's thoughts? Can you see how tight Solène's grip is on him?"

Her grandmother's face tensed as she nodded. "Yes," she said softly. "But it's not right. I shouldn't. His thoughts should be his own."

"My thoughts haven't been my own for a very long time. Camille, please," Zéolie begged as her grandmother's resolve wavered. "His thoughts could unlock how to stop all this. If we can't see Solène's thoughts, we might be able to figure out what she's doing through Julien's. If she's controlling him, he's as dangerous as she is."

Her grandmother was quiet as she considered Zéolie's reasoning. Silence engulfed the two of them as Zéolie waited. After several long moments, Camille finally spoke. "I'll do it."

"How can I help?" Zéolie asked.

Camille gave her a wan smile. "You can't, *chérie*. It's too dangerous. He won't notice me in his thoughts since I'm unfamiliar to him. You'd draw his attention. And your mother's."

"Won't she notice you?"

"Probably, but there's nothing she can do about that. She can block her thoughts from me, but she can't touch me," Camille answered with a twinkle in her shimmering eyes. Pausing a moment, her expression grew more serious. "If that demon is controlling him, his thoughts could be terrifying. Are you sure you want to see them?"

"No," Zéolie said, "but we have no choice."

Camille nodded and closed her eyes. Her rippling form began to flicker as she sent her energy into the thoughts of her grandson. Zéolie feared losing the connection completely as Camille's image became dangerously faint. Tingling hands and a pressure in Zéolie's chest told her Mama Nell and Mother Micheaux were listening and sending more energy to her in case she needed to pull Camille back.

The flickering became erratic as Camille strengthened the connection to Julien. Images began to flash between Zéolie and her grandmother as though they were ghosts on a pane of glass, transparent, but definitely there. They flashed rapidly from one to another with no rhyme or reason at all. If Julien's mind was as frantic as his thoughts, he was quickly losing his sanity. Feelings, intense and dark, accompanied the rapid-fire pictures. Zéolie braced herself for what came hurtling at her.

A cabin in a burning swamp. Confusion and questions. Thinking there was something he should know but couldn't figure out. A feeling of being watched.

A woman with red lips and long crossed legs twirling a strand of hair around her finger. The same woman watching without emotion as a burst of energy shot from his hand and sent a ragged girl through a wall into a puddle of her own blood. A sickening nausea, but a focused intention to get it right the next time.

Celeste Marchon running her finger across the back of his shoulders and laughing softly. Her flirtatious pout as she twirled a long curl around a graceful finger. Celeste's thoughts and her genuine adoration. Softness in his heart, but confusion about what he wanted. Love, but a sense of betrayal.

Zéolie looking over the balcony at him, smiling as her long black hair slid down in front of her shoulders. Desire and self-doubt collided. Walking with her arm through his in the Marchon courtyard. Heart pounding with nervousness, but certain of what he wanted. A carriage turning a corner as she leaned in and kissed Louis. Julien's heart ripping wide open as electricity and rage consumed him.

Darkness and a clearing in the woods. A small dilapidated hut, with a smoldering fire in front and trinkets in the trees. Confusion and compulsion. Mental and physical exhaustion.

Underneath it all, the low menacing laugh and repulsive sing-song that Zéolie knew far too well.

"*Enough!*" Zéolie shouted over the echoing laughter. "No more! Let him go, Camille!"

Emotions and images evaporated as Camille's form solidified. She was haggard and strained from the exertion, but the connection wasn't lost. "I warned you," she whispered. "I tried to tell you."

"I know," Zéolie said, her heart racing with the influx of energy and fear at what she witnessed. "You were right. I didn't want to believe you, but you were right." Zéolie sighed trying to will the weight of her brother's thoughts off her shoulders. "He—he killed that girl, didn't he?"

Camille lowered her eyes. Tears shone on her lashes. "He did. And I don't think she was the only one. There were too many thoughts coming too fast for me to show them all to you." A sob shook her as she spoke, "He's gone, Zéolie. That poor boy is hers and he doesn't even realize it."

"*No!*" Zéolie screamed. "I won't believe that!"

"Gone. He's too far gone," Camille sobbed, dangerously close to slipping back into the mire of her own guilt.

Zéolie sent a shockwave of energy at her grandmother as pain shot through her heart. "*Stop it!*" Camille was rocked by the burst, turning a shocked stare at her granddaughter. "Don't you dare give up on him!" Zéolie snarled. "There's love in his heart still. You felt it, too. He's not gone!"

Slowly, Camille nodded as Zéolie caught her breath. Anger and panic surged with the energy coursing through her.

"Listen to me. All of you!" Zéolie shouted. "This isn't Julien's fault and we can't leave him to that—that *witch*! Sentenced to die for the crime of being born, then sent away. Rejected by the only friends he had. No one to tell him what he really is. No one to teach him to control his thoughts and power. Scared and alone. Julien isn't to blame for this—*we are! All of us!*" Stunned silence consumed her as Camille, Nell, and Mother Micheaux wallowed in their guilt. "You can all go crawling into your own self-righteousness if you want to, but I refuse to let that demon take my brother down with her!" Panting, and emotionally spent, Zéolie began to weaken her hold on Camille.

Her grandmother's edges began to fade into a fine mist as Nell and Mother Micheaux fought to push more energy to Zéolie. Once more, she visualized her chest opening and drawing in vibrant white energy from the nun and priestess. As she did, Camille began to ripple back into her more solid form, but tears were streaming down her shimmering face.

"Camille," Zéolie whispered, "he's your grandson. Please don't abandon him now. There has to be a way."

"She's so strong, Zéolie." Camille's voice was more thought than sound.

Zéolie's heart ached for her. "None of us can take Solène down alone," she said gently.

Camille lifted her eyes to meet Zéolie's. "And if this doesn't work?"

Fear crept into Zéolie's thoughts as the answer to that question materialized. Knowing she didn't have the luxury of doubt, she forced it aside and answered, "Then, I'll take down Julien." The words hung in the air between them, ringing with determination. Camille stared at her granddaughter's resolute face and nodded. "Where is he now?" Zéolie asked.

Camille closed her eyes and flickered for an instant before replying, "Horseback. On the river road."

Mother Micheaux's voice rang over their heads. "The Haydels. Solène's bringing him home."

Zéolie's dark eyes narrowed. "Then we're running out of time." She paused and softened her expression towards her grandmother. "You've done so much that I hate to ask more of you," she said softly. "We won't have time for a seance out there and I'll need your help."

Camille straightened her spine, standing tall and confident, and released her fear and guilt to the ether. "You'll have it. You always do."

CHAPTER
TWENTY-FIVE

Dark hair lay plastered in sweat on Julien's forehead as he rode slumped in the saddle, exhausted more from the constant barrage from the voice than the ride itself. His body begged for him to stop, and even his horse seemed to resist every step forward, but neither could do anything about it. They were being pulled onward by something stronger than man or beast. Fading rays of light barely illuminated the dirt path stretching out interminably in front of them. Daytime sounds of birds and scurrying animals ceased, giving way to the night noises of crickets and frogs along the riverbank singing in harmony with the churning water. Step by agonizing step, the horse carried her tortured rider down a path she could barely see.

With the last of the light came a new direction, one that neither was any more willing to accept, but couldn't resist. Sliding and scattering dirt and pebbles down the embankment, the horse left the road. Eyes frantic and ears laid back in fear, she trudged against her will into the dark tree line. With no worn path, branches Julien couldn't see slashed him across the face forcing him to lie against the horse's strong neck as she carried him into the depths of the thick woods, tentatively picking her way through the dense underbrush. Still the voice laughed and sang, pushing his sanity further and further out of his grasp.

Stumbling over fallen trees and struggling through thickets of thorns, the mare pushed on into the blackness. Julien wound the leather reins tight around his wrists as his body began to fail him. Weakness flooded every muscle, threatening to pull him from the horse. Heels of his boots wedged deep in the stirrups held his legs against the horse's flanks as the wound reins held his hands to the saddle horn. What little strength he had left was directed at staying on his mount, leaving his mind a playground for the voice and her whims.

Time lost cohesion in the dark depths, swimming between the present trek and past memories. Images flashed, constantly bombarding his tormented mind. Underneath it all, night sounds blended with a soft wind moaning through the tops of the trees in an eerie chorus. The sing-song of the voice began to change as the chorus around him built, blending her voice with nature's chorus in a rich minor key. Same familiar song, but sinister in the new arrangement. Words slipped in and out of the droning hum until finally, as the horse pushed deeper, they became clear.

> *Au clair de la lune,*
> *Mon ami Pierrot,*
> *Prête-moi ta plume*
> *Pour écrire un mot.*
> *Ma chandelle est morte,*
> *Je n´ai plus de feu,*
> *Ouvre-moi ta porte,*
> *Pour l´amour de Dieu.*

Haunting and beautiful, Julien knew the song, but didn't know why. It was simple. A child's song. Had he heard it in Paris? Likely, but that wasn't the feeling attached to it. There was familiarity and comfort in the song as if it was connected to him somehow.

As he struggled to place the song through the rapid-fire images, the trees parted in front of him. Branches no longer scraped against him as the horse took her last careful steps before stopping and sinking to her knees. Unwinding the reins and releasing his heels, Julien slid from the mare's back and onto his stomach in the soft leaf litter on the ground.

Julien strained his eyes to see his surroundings in the clearing, but the darkness was complete. "Where am I?" His own raspy voice startled him.

"*Home*," the voice said gently then resumed her song.

On the ground a few yards in front of him, a flame glowed dimly in deep greens and purples before growing enough to illuminate the clearing. The brightness blinded Julien's eyes so accustomed to the blackness of the woods. Blinking hard and fast, he tried to bring everything into focus in the unholy light. There was no warmth to the flame that flickered in the remains of a campfire in front of a ragged hut. Strange light danced in the trees giving a sense of motion to the talismans and trinkets hanging in the low branches. Feathers bound to bones, other bones wrapped with beaded leather cord, dangled overhead. Tiny dolls with fragments of cloth, feathers, small bones, and other odd things attached to them hung by their necks from the limbs.

"I don't understand," Julien whispered.

As the words left his mouth, a figure materialized in the flickering green shadows, transparent but clear. A woman with long black hair cradled a small bundle, rocking it and dancing slowly around the flame. The song in his head lost its hollowness as it flowed through the space in front of him to the figure who began to sing to the child in her arms. After a moment, she raised her eyes from the baby then looked down at Julien and smiled.

"Mother?" he asked, breathlessly struggling to his knees. The woman nodded and went back to dancing with her baby. The image began to fray and fade. "No! Wait! Don't go!"

"Hush, *chérie*," the voice in his head said. "There's more to see."

It was the same voice. "It's been you all along?" Julien asked her.

"Yes, child," she answered gently.

"Why didn't you tell me? Why hide who you are?" he asked.

"You weren't ready," she replied simply.

"Ready for what?"

A low chuckle from his mother. "To know the truth. For battle."

Julien shook his head, trying to force thoughts into place as they swirled relentlessly. "I—I don't understand."

"Shh, *chérie*. You will."

The hideous green light around him began to gather into shape again as the image shifted. His mother holding the child again, this time frightened and angry as the baby was taken from her by a tall well-dressed man. Rage and tears flooded him as he felt her emotions along with the vision. More figures emerged from the shadows and brought her to the ground. Figures he didn't know, except for one. Mother Micheaux.

None of it made sense to him as his mother fought against her attackers and screamed at the man standing stoically above her, "*No! You took one child from me! I won't let you take Julien, too!*" It was no use. She was overpowered but got one massive burst of energy into the chest of one of the women, a priestess, holding her down. The woman staggered back as the image faded.

Green mist swirled and twisted into another image. Mother Micheaux and a different man, his face full of fear and disgust. "This is your nephew's mess, Jean-Jacques," the nun said. "It's his son and that makes it your mess, too. She can't have that child. God knows what she'd turn him into or what she'd use him for. She'll take down anyone in her way to get him back. You know what you have to do." The mother superior's expression was menacing and fierce.

"I—I can't kill a child," the man said, his voice trembling.

"It's not a *choice*," she hissed. "Do it." The man nodded solemnly, and the nun glared at him one last time before turning on her heel as the vision faded.

Another image began to take its place. Zéolie's dark eyes and long black hair as she smiled up at the tall stoic man, who wrapped his arms around her and kissed her forehead. "I'll always need you, Papa," she said, her voice echoing in the memory. Something struck him about the image. He knew the man from before. The one who took the baby from his mother. But there was something else. Something about Zéolie. As he struggled to put it together, the images layered, and his mother was standing beside her smiling at him. Her eyes, her smile, her hair. Her tall grace and strength mirrored in the young woman next to her. Zéolie was the other child the man took from his mother. Zéolie. His—

"Sister," his mother's voice finished the thought for him. "Zéolie Cheval is my daughter."

"But—she can't be." Nausea washed over him as he realized the woman he'd lost his heart to and fantasized about was his own sister. "She said she didn't know you. She lied to me?"

"No, *chérie*. She didn't know a Marie Haydel because there is no Marie Haydel. The Haydel whelp never married me, but I never wanted you to know yourself as the bastard child you are, so I gave you his name. And the name of the one man I loved. The man who took everything from me, including my heart. Your sister knows me for who I really am—Solène Marie Cheval."

Julien reeled and collapsed onto the ground underneath him, face down in the leaves and sobbed. "You *lied* to me! All these years! You *lied!*"

"To protect you, *chérie*. From them," she spat, recreating the image of the ones who took him from her the first time. "They took you once, and I had to fight to get you back from the Haydels. The weak fool Jean-Jacques couldn't do what the mother superior ordered, so you lived, but they could never know that. They'd hunt you down like they are now. *They know who you are, Julien.* They're coming for you like they came for me. Your sister's coming with them."

"No!" Julien shouted, scrambling to his hands and knees and backing away from the image in front of him. "Zéolie won't hurt me. She can't. I'm stronger than her! She can't do what I can do!"

His mother raged as the images reverberated with her wrath. "*Foolish child!* She's stronger than you'll ever be! *She* can control the power that races in her blood!"

Shame at his own failures consumed him as his mother's disappointment rained down on his heart and mind.

"She could've had the world at her feet with me, but the little bitch refused," Solène's mad tirade raged on around him as the images faded and changed again. A cabin on stilts in a flaming swamp emerged from the mist. Julien knew this place. He'd seen it in his dreams. "I couldn't force her to come to me. Those idiots saw to that, so she had to come on her own."

A sharp cackle, then a sultry laugh as she continued her raving. "But I had something they didn't count on. Her precious Officer Louis Soucier." Mist shifted again and Julien saw the man from the carriage surrounded by candles, unconscious and bleeding as his mother ran a long finger down Louis' bare chest and ran her tongue along red grinning lips. Another wave of nausea as Julien realized what his mother had done. "*Still* the little fool refused me!" Solène shrieked.

"You're mad," Julien said, shaking uncontrollably as he tried to get to his feet. A hard slap landed on his face, knocking him to the ground.

"No, child, you're the mad one if you don't think she'll kill you like *she killed me!*"

"Zéolie couldn't do that. You're too strong." Sweat stood out in cold beads all over his skin and his breath was shallow and fast.

"See for yourself what your precious sister can do," Solène snarled.

Desperately trying to stay conscious, he watched the trees spinning around him as another image began to form. Julien stood outside the cabin at the edge of the clearing in the swamp watching his mother dancing on the rooftop, precarious as she spun and laughed. Below her, Zéolie held her hands out toward one of the towering cypress trees that burned in a ring of fire surrounding them. With a deep groan and deafening cracks, the mighty tree lifted out of the marsh and hovered a moment before Zéolie's hands whipped toward the cabin, sending the massive thing hurtling at Solène. In a shower of sparks, the tree incinerated his mother as she tumbled from the roof to a lifeless heap at the foot of one of the stilts with flames consuming her body. Zéolie's face was triumphant as she reached for Louis, kissing him as Julien's mother burned.

Blind rage exploded in his chest as his mind finally broke under the strain of the images and fury of his mother. Electricity sparked along his skin, white-hot and stinging. Solène's voice shook the ground, driving the madness of her son as deep as she could, securing her hold on his shattered mind.

"That *demon* girl took your mother from you! The only woman who ever really loved you, protected you, fought for you! The little witch couldn't share the power she possesses and killed your mother to keep that power for herself. And now she knows what you can do. *She's coming, Julien! She's coming to kill you, too!'*

Julien's face that was contorted through the onslaught of images and shrieking eased into a sightless glare as his mother settled herself into the depths of his mind. With nothing left to fight for and his strength completely gone, Solène's broken child gave himself over to the control of his mother's power. The corner of his lip curled into a satisfied grin as his body sat on his haunches next to the hut to wait for his sister to come.

TWENTY-SIX

Hoofbeats kept time with pounding hearts as scattered pebbles skittered across the river road. Beside the motley crew of travelers, the mighty river slid silently by, racing away from them toward the sea as though fearful of what lay in wait upstream. Still the horses charged on toward unknown dangers and familiar enemies. Fading afternoon light washed the dirt path in deep oranges and golden yellows, cheerful under different circumstances. To the weary riders, the colors only meant that time was racing faster than they were.

Pressing on in collective silence, each was consumed with their own thoughts. Three rehearsed words that held power to those who knew them and how to wield them. One reviewed facts that pieced together a fearsome puzzle. One, a boy, rode in a silence that was complete—terrified but upright as he rode point toward danger he could never imagine. Time taunted them, slipping through their fingers as the sun melted into the horizon. Shadows of the thickening trees stretched lazily across the road, shrouding the way forward. Onward they coursed as a thin crescent of moon shared the sky with the sinking sun before taking control of the night.

Blackness settled heavily over the Louisiana wilds, plunging the travelers into darkness that ran deeper than the sky. Fear pricked at them as their destination neared but remained hidden in the deep forest ahead. Crouching in the depths, a creature lurked more dangerous than the beasts of the black heart of the swamp. Intuition screamed at them to run, yet duty and determination spurred them ever onwards.

Pushing her horse harder, Mother Micheaux overtook Squire at the front of the pack. Giving him a folded paper, she put her hand on his head in blessing before sending him on to the Haydel plantation. Watching his horse disappear into the night, she sent words on his heels to shield him from harm as the boy brought warning to the family. She could only hope it wasn't too late. Warning was weak atonement for the sin she had forced on them decades before.

Doubling back, the mother superior pulled silently alongside the others and slowed them to a walk with a raised hand. With the hooves of their mounts quieted on the dirt road, sounds of night surrounded them. Crickets chirped in the reeds and underbrush. Night birds took flight with soft wingbeats overhead. Frogs croaked in rhythmic echoes in the leaf litter. Cool evening air washed over their road-worn faces. Serenity masked the sinister.

Even in the relative peace of the night, electricity skipped along Zéolie's skin, growing stronger with each step of her horse. The nun and priestess felt it, too, as the three women exchanged wordless glances in the dark. Sensing the anxiety of their riders, the horses twitched and snorted, resisting heels in their flanks urging them on.

In the dim moonlight, Mother Micheaux pointed to a scarred patch of land where a horse had skidded down the embankment. A nod to Zéolie and the girl turned her wrist to gather energy in the palm of her hand, taking the shape of a ball of pale blue moonlight. Enough to illuminate what it was near, but not bright enough to be noticed deeper in the trees. Softly blowing on it, she sent the light drifting above the ruts to the edge of the trees where it hovered in front of freshly broken branches.

Louis looked at Mother Micheaux as she raised the reins to urge the horse forward. His voice, the slightest whisper, cut through the quiet of the night. "He'll hear us coming."

With a nod, Mother Micheaux, Mama Nell, and Zéolie raised their hands, palms outward, and closed their eyes. For an instant, Louis saw a flicker of silver light surround the four horses and riders. Camille would shield their approach through the brush. Sounds of the horses and riders muffled as though the travelers were underwater. Distant and thick, then deathly quiet. Moving forward into the brush, branches snapped and scraped without a sound. Hooves stepped through thickets silently. In the riders' ears, heartbeats thundered.

Single file, the horses followed the signs of the one who went before them. Their riders' hearts raced as they kept a snail's pace through the wood, ever wary of what lay ahead. With each step closer to their destination, the air hummed harder with electricity that stung and burned Zéolie's skin. She winced with the pain but made no sound. More agonizing silent steps forward before the silence was finally broken. The low laugh that until now had only haunted Zéolie's mind echoed softly through the trees. Louis' eyes widened as he scanned the treetops for the witch he knew too well. Nothing. Only the laugh.

As they listened, the laugh faded and the sounds of night once more surrounded them, but this time in a chorus of soft song. After a moment, the voice joined in a rich minor key, gentle but eerie. The forest itself seemed to find the harmony and add depth to the music around them.

Zéolie cringed as she thought of the last time she had heard her mother's song in the deep swamp. Louis shuddered, while the priestess and mother superior mouthed words of protection. If they could hear Solène's singing, they were close enough to be in very real danger.

Mother Micheaux inched the horses forward, sending ancient words before her. Mama Nell sent prayers to the ancestors and loa, begging protection against the evil in the darkness. Zéolie pushed mental tendrils out, searching for Julien's thoughts. Louis watched, once more feeling useless against a force he was ill-equipped to face.

Mother Micheaux's hand raised to stop the horses as she scanned the woods ahead. Familiarity flooded her. With a glance at Nell, she knew why. Twenty-one years ago, they had stood in the same place listening to Solène singing to the baby in her arms. Peering through the trees, they could see a faint flicker of strange light. It moved like fire but danced in shades of deep greens and purples, casting bizarre shadows in the tree branches overhead. Whatever that light was, maybe it was enough to see what was in the clearing before it saw them.

The riders eased themselves from the saddles of their mounts as the three women whispered protections into the velvet ears of the faithful horses. Steeling themselves for what lay ahead, the travelers ventured forward on foot. Steps became painfully slow as fear oozed from their pores with each move they made closer to their reckoning.

Mother Micheaux reached the clearing first, stopping just shy of the ring of trees to remain hidden. Overhead, trinkets and dolls danced in the gentle breeze. Strange things like scraps of fabric, tufts of hair, and chicken bones were attached to them with straight pins.

Looking up at them, the nun was captivated by one of the dolls. Others in nearby branches stared blankly ahead. This one, with eyes of beaded black glass, seemed to look down at her, amused. Strange flickering light glinted off the beaded eye- or had it winked?

Pulling her attention away, Mother Micheaux surveyed the branches around her. Charms tied to them seemed to be at different heights depending on the branch, but all of them were in a line mirroring the shape of the clearing. Solène had created a ring of protection around her camp.

A thin, aging finger pointed up at the trinkets as the others followed her gaze. Magical playthings dangling in the sweeping limbs. Silent nods from the women, and more silent words flowed from lips that tried not to tremble with the icy fear they felt. As the words flowed, trees began to shimmer and fade, only pale remnants of the trunks remained between the travelers and the clearing. Still Solène sang, seeming not to notice the transformation.

Louis braced for an attack from Solène or Julien, but none came. Only then did he realize that the transparent trees they saw were still solid to anyone but the four of them. Otherwise, the witch would have reacted.

Through the ghosts of the forest, they could see the source of the odd light in the campfire. It burned but didn't consume anything. Glowed, but gave no heat. Flames of purple and green entwined like lovers around kindling that didn't ignite. All the while, it cast shadows on the trees and the hut at the far side.

Against the hut, a figure crouched soaked in sweat, eyes glowing green with the reflected light. Zéolie put her hand over her mouth to stifle a sob as she recognized the shell of her brother trembling, but not with fear. The snarl on his lips betrayed the pent-up energy he was waiting to unleash. His humanity was gone. No sign of the bashful, innocent boy that shifted his weight uncertainly on her front step in his search for his mother. He'd found her and was paying for it with his life.

I won't attack him, Zéolie thought. *We let this happen. I can't destroy him for something he didn't do.* Slowly, she straightened her spine in determination to end the nightmare once and for all, hands clenched at her side. He was his mother's physical connection to the world, and a dangerous one, so walking out there like her father did years ago wasn't an option. There was too much power with mother and son together to risk that. Before she did anything else, she needed to find out just what she was dealing with. Zéolie brought her hand to her mouth, then pushed her palm to one of the trees on the far side of the hut.

"Julien?" her voice said gently from across the clearing.

His dark head snapped around to the sound of the voice, like an animal catching the scent of its prey. Raising up on his haunches slightly, he cocked his head to listen. The snarling grin on his face darkened as his mother's song faded into the night.

Once more, but to the other side of him, Zéolie threw her voice. "Julien, I'm not here to hurt you."

Julien wheeled around, confused, but still hunting the voice.

To the far side once more, "I'm sorry I hurt you, but you don't understand."

Julien's eyes searched the clearing as he realized the voice wasn't attached to its owner. Zéolie backed into the shadows behind a trunk of one of the ghostly trees, but his eyes locked on her.

"Sister," he hissed, his voice strained with the pain of holding back the energy threatening to burst out of him.

"She told you?" Zéolie asked, her voice connected to her once more.

He nodded as though the lifting and lowering of his own head was tremendous effort. His body uncurled, standing up to face the voice in the woods.

"Everything," Julien growled. With the flame between them casting dark dancing shadows, his trembling was exaggerated to the point of being grotesque. His body was upright, but still tensed for attack, twitching under the power that built in his veins. Every muscle coiled and waiting for the blessed release.

Zéolie glanced at the mother superior and the priestess whose mouths moved constantly in silent chants of protection. Through the ghostly blur of the trees, she could see a hand with bloody finger-nails rise, extended straight out in front of the trembling body. The palm pulled in toward the rigid shoulder as if he were cocking a gun. Zéolie watched the intricacies of the movements, the flexing and relaxing of muscles like one would watch the slow perfect move-ments of a ballet.

A thick trunk stood between her body and the palm as she watched, but dark eyes locked as if the tree wasn't there at all. An instant later, it wasn't.

Julien's hand shot forward with blinding speed as electricity fired from it, shattering the illusion of the transparent forest and splintering the tree. Limbs exploded overhead, crashing down through the canopy as the others dove away from their massive crushing weight. Under a hailstorm of raining shards, Zéolie lay face-down in the underbrush.

Mama Nell left the mystic words to Mother Micheaux and raced to the girl, skidding onto her knees bedside her. Before Nell's body stopped, it was thrown in a wild arc above the green fire and into the wall of the hut. Liquid grace flowed into a heap of scarves and unconsciousness.

As the priestess sank to the ground, Julien took cautious steps toward Zéolie, rolling slowly from heel to toe. His face shifted from anger to concern in an internal battle with his mother's agenda and his own feelings for his sister. Snarling lips contrasted soft pleading eyes. Though his own mind struggled valiantly, Solène's rage overpowered him.

Louis scrambled to his feet, climbing over jagged limbs to get to Zéolie, but was hit in the gut with something he couldn't see that knocked the wind out of him. He was thrown to the ground behind a large, leaf-filled branch. Stunned, Louis looked around and saw the mother superior's hand outstretched toward him, holding him in place.

Confused, his dark blue eyes searched her face for an answer. The nun's expression softened in apology, then hardened giving warning for him to stay down. Once he acquiesced, Mother Micheaux's thin hand lowered releasing her hold on him. Refusing to acknowledge his uselessness, Louis watched every move Julien made and scanned the trees above for signs of Solène. He had no idea what he could do against any of them and knew Mother Micheaux would stop him before he had a chance to try, but maybe he could at least give warning.

Zéolie's breathing became less labored as she pulled strength from the space and energy around her. Lifting her body to hands and knees, she pulled embedded shards of wood from her arms. Blood trickled down unchecked from the wounds. Seeing her rising strength, Julien stopped his advance. Cautious, he put one foot behind him, planting his feet for retaliation from her. Zéolie eased herself to standing, stacking her vertebrae up to their full height.

Hands, palms out at her side, gathered electricity that pooled there waiting for release. In her ears, Zéolie's heart thrummed. Tears settled in dark eyes as she gazed at the tortured soul watching her like a wary animal. "Julien," she whispered, "don't do this." His eyes narrowed at the sound of her voice. "Please, Julien. I don't want to hurt you."

Solène's laugh cracked over their heads. Julien cringed, crouching and searching the tree canopy for the witch. "*Foolish child!*" their mother shrieked.

Chills raced down Zéolie's spine. It was one thing to push to the back of her mind the relentless hollow laugh that seemed so far away, but hearing the words reverberating through the clearing made her stomach sink.

Solène's wrath shook the forest floor under their feet. "You think *you* can hurt him?" More laughter. "You inherited more of your father's foolishness than I thought! The blood on Julien's hands makes him stronger than you'll ever be, my beautiful weakling!"

Zéolie shook her head, silvery tears falling on her cheeks. "No," she croaked. "I won't believe that. I'll never believe he killed in cold blood."

Julien's face twitched, torn between his need for Solène's approval and his own conscience that was determined to keep pushing itself to the surface, gasping for air under the flood of attack from Solène. The momentary glimmer of the true Julien wasn't lost on Zéolie, who seized it.

"You didn't want to kill those girls, did you?" she asked softly, still holding the energy in her hands at the ready. "No one taught you how to control your power. No one told you anything." Her brother's eyes rested on her face, but his body tensed. "I'm sorry, Julien. I was afraid of what you were. That you were like *her.*"

Solène snarled, but Zéolie didn't back down.

From the corner of her eye, she could see the mother superior moving silently through the tree line to the rear of Julien. She had to keep her mother's and brother's attention until the nun could get in position. "Solène's own hatred and madness consumes her. I was afraid it would happen to you." Julien's face twitched again, but he was silent, so she kept pushing. "But I was *wrong*, Julien. I shouldn't have let you go like that. I knew what was happening to you, and I didn't tell you. I should've gone after you. I should've explained."

Julien's eyes rolled back in his head as Solène loosened her possession of him to unleash on her daughter. An unseen hand slapped Zéolie hard across the face. A crimson stream ran from Zéolie's lip where Solène made contact, but she stayed on her feet. Scratches streaked across her pale face, opening faint blue veins. Blood seeped through the cloth of her bodice from clawed scratches down her back. Teeth clenched, she endured the pain.

Louis tried to get to his feet, but as he did, he caught the angry glare of Mother Micheaux and dropped back down fuming. He couldn't stand Zéolie being abused but knew if the mother superior wanted him out of sight, she had a reason and could make sure he stayed down.

As much as she was determined not to engage her mother's attack and provoke Julien, Zéolie reached a breaking point. "*Enough, Solène!*" Her right hand shot straight up and fired a burst of white lightning into the air. Knowing Solène could be anywhere, it was literally a shot in the dark. Her mother's low laugh mocked her effort. "Damn it," Zéolie growled. There was only one way she was going to get to Solène, and she wasn't about to unleash on her brother if she could help it.

Julien stood trembling at the edge of the fire, watching Zéolie take on his mother. Even with the blackening bruise forming on her jawbone and the claw marks on her cheeks, she was powerful. Julien's body contorted as he struggled against Solène's mental attack as his sister withstood her physical one. Hands that had been flexing and unsure were thrust straight down at his side. Knuckle by knuckle, they curled into fists as energy gathered there.

Zéolie couldn't see the power surging in his fingers but could feel it being pulled away from the space around her. Still, her energy held fast in her own hands. Unsure what Julien was planning, she braced for another shot, knowing she may fare as badly as the tree. Behind her brother, the mother superior crept into the clearing, poised to take him from behind. A flicker of Zéolie's focus on the nun gave her away.

Julien turned as his hands shot straight out to his sides, splitting the power gathered there in two directions. One burst struck Mother Micheaux, whose hand went up to deflect. Even though she managed to send his shot wide, there was enough force to knock her off her feet. Another burst let loose on Zéolie, whose hands flew in front of her, crossed at the wrist, ricocheting Julien's energy off her own.

Panicking, Julien began to pull electricity for another attack when Mother Micheaux regained her feet. Just as he took aim at his sister, his left foot was yanked out from under him, catching Julien unawares and throwing him to the ground. Zéolie's eyes searched for what caused it and saw the flicker of a sparking whip in the mother superior's hand that evaporated before it fully materialized. As much as the nun had wanted Julien dead as a boy, Zéolie knew she wasn't going to harm him now if she could take him down another way. Even with his direct attacks on them, both women remained on the defensive.

Once more, Solène's voice rang through the trees. *"Kill them, Julien!* Start with this one!" she shrieked, raising the unconscious body of Mama Nell to her feet, then lifting her slightly above the ground. The graceful priestess hung there like a morbid marionette, arms held straight out by her elbows, wrists dangling loosely below them, bracelets glinting in the purple and green flame. Her head wrapped in a crimson tignon rolled around on a neck too limp to hold it. Legs hung beneath skirts and scarves covered in dead leaves and twigs.

A ripple moved through the priestess, slight at first. Then, Nell's body convulsed violently as it vomited hundreds of rusted straight pins onto the dirt floor of the clearing. Blood streamed from burgundy lips and ran down her chin onto the pins beneath her in thick crimson threads.

"*Now, Julien!*" Solène ordered. "Do it! Send her to her filthy mother!"

"No!" Zéolie screamed. "No, Julien! You're not Solène's slave. You're not a killer! That's *not who you are!*"

Julien watched Nell dangle and sway as Solène held her aloft. Head cocked to the side, he flattened one hand out and gathered energy once more.

"Don't do this, Julien. Please don't do this," his sister begged frantically. "Mama Nell can teach you control. She taught me. Nell didn't come here to hurt you. She came here to protect me and *help you.*"

Tears ran down her face as she spoke. Unspoken words pleaded in her mind, *Camille, she needs you! Shield her!* A flash of silver light that could have been mistaken for a play of the eerie flames sparked around Nell then vanished. Camille had heard her granddaughter's plea.

Julien's hand cocked at his shoulder once more, but instead of sending the blast into Nell, he sent it above her head, severing the invisible cords holding her up. His other hand went out and caught her body and held it inches above the ground before gently lowering her down.

"*Useless boy!*" Solène roared and slapped her son sprawling into the dirt.

"No," he snarled. "She's done nothing to me. My fight isn't with her." On hands and knees, his eyes found the mother superior at the edge of the tree line. "*You,*" he growled through clenched teeth. "You ordered them to *kill me!*" Raising up to his full height, his hands met at his chest, blue sparks jumping from one palm to the other.

Mother Micheaux stood to face him. "She showed you," she whispered. His narrowed eyes confirmed it. "Yes," she said gently. "It was wrong, and I will live and die with that sin on my soul. But you don't have to die with this on yours. The young man I met was kind and loving. Not this. Not his mother's weapon. You can stop all this, Julien. Stop *her*."

Julien watched her talk, holding the energy between his hands at the ready. Measuring her words. Weighing them for truth. "Stop her," he whispered. "Why?"

"Because," Zéolie said as Julien whipped around to face her, "she'll use you to kill again and again. She killed Nell's mother, my father, Father Antoine, Vernand, and a young nun named Angelie. All because they tried to protect me from her. Protect me from *becoming* her. And Celeste." Julien's eyes flashed at the mention of the name. Another twitch as he fought off Solène's insistent mental barrage. "Julien, she tried to kill Celeste. She'll do it again."

Julien's face contorted to pained sadness.

Zéolie's voice dropped to barely a whisper. "You know that, don't you? You know Solène wants to hurt Celeste because Celeste loves you."

Tears gathered in his dark eyes, huddling together on the edges of his lashes. "Loves me?" he asked. "She can't love me. Not like this."

"No, not like this. She loves who you really are. Loving, kind, bashful, and handsome. This monster isn't you. *This* is Solène."

Her mother lashed out at both of them, knocking Zéolie to the ground and wrapping invisible fingers around Julien's throat. Tightening her grip, Solène lifted him to the balls of his feet as he choked with a sickening gurgle.

"*Kill her*, Julien," Solène growled. "The little Marchon wench doesn't love you. Your sister lies to save her own skin. *Kill her!*" As his consciousness began to waver, she released him.

Gasping for air, Julien staggered close to the fire. Eyes narrowing, he stared into the flames that began to shift and take shape. Once more, the image of his mother on the roof of the swamp cabin materialized, followed by Zéolie lifting the massive tree out of the mire and hurtling it at Solène. Mother Micheaux, Julien, and Zéolie watched as Solène fell in a burning, lifeless heap at the base of the cabin stilts while his sister relished her victory.

What little color was left under the streaked blood and bruises drained from Zéolie's face as Julien's raging eyes met hers.

"*No!*" she screamed scrambling to her feet. Her voice cracked with fear. "That's not what happened! I didn't kill her!" she shrieked, panicking as Julien once more turned his wrath on his sister.

"She's right, Julien." Mother Micheaux said, taking cautious steps closer to him. "She didn't kill Solène."

"*Lies!*" Solène hissed.

"Julien, she can make those flames say anything she wants. Solène's power-hungry rage killed her." The mother superior's words were measured and soft. One more step forward. A nod to Louis over Zéolie's shoulder.

Louis crept around the shattered corpse of the tree and inched toward the three people standing in the middle of the clearing. Julien's gaze flitted from Zéolie to the mother superior, trying to decide who to believe. The shadows of the flames and the proximity of the women hid Louis' advance as he crept feet from Zéolie. Whatever the mother superior was planning was putting him dangerously close to a loose cannon.

Zéolie's mind raced as she tried to think of a way to make Julien see the truth. Words, like flames, could say anything.

"Zéolie," Camille's voice said, "show him the truth."

How? Zéolie asked. *Only Louis knows the truth.*

"Child, build a bridge."

"It's time you saw the truth, brother," Zéolie said, calm on the outside as her insides trembled. Her arms rose straight out to her sides, then just above her shoulders. Julien was yanked forward until his forehead met her left palm. Louis did the same on her right side.

A silver flash surged outward from her chest to the tips of her fingers as Camille solidified the bridge between the two minds. Mother Micheaux watched as Julien and Louis were held transfixed, eyes staring blankly ahead as memories were shared.

Through the ring of trees, Solène shrieked vile curses as she fought to sever the tie Camille created. Unable to combat her own mother and daughter, Solène turned her wrath on the mother superior. For every strike Solène managed to land, Mother Micheaux matched her blow for blow in a stagnant duel of electricity and rage. Still the trio in the center remained statues as memories traveled through Zéolie's body.

Energy began to build wildly above the storm of magical volleys. Thunder rolled in the darkness and lightning flashed. Still they battled, the nun sending shots in broad arcs covering as much of the clearing as she could, and Solène driving her attack more directly. With one hand holding off Solène, Mother Micheaux sent a gentle push of power to the unconscious priestess. In the energy, she sent a message, hoping as Mama Nell came to, she'd be able to understand what was happening quick enough to stay out of harm's way.

"So, you're still a coward, Mother!" Solène mocked. "Couldn't kill him then and can't kill him now! So high and mighty behind your veil, aren't you? The black hides your sins from others, Mother, but *I* can still see them!"

"You're wrong, witch. It's not cowardice that stops me now," the mother superior spat as she sent a volley of sparking arrows into the night. "I've confessed my sin and am serving my penance."

Solène's invisible hand landed squarely on the side of Mother Micheaux's face as she cackled. "You think confession will wipe away what you've done? There's no place in Heaven for the likes of us." She laughed as the battle raged on.

Julien's face began to shift from the blank stare of the trance to deep sorrow as the memories reached their end. Finally, the silver flash rippled through Zéolie's arms back to her chest once more. Her hands released and her heart pounded. Strong shoulders slumped and deep blue veins streaked across her face as exhaustion washed over her. Louis' face drained and veins appeared beneath his sandy stubble as he sank to the ground.

Julien swayed, but kept his feet. Slowly, he turned his gaze on Zéolie. "My god," he whispered. "You didn't kill her. You *died* to stop her." His sister nodded weakly. "And Louis," Julien's voice cracked as tears rained from broken eyes. "He—" The rest died on his lips as his own conscience and emotions flooded back into him. "What have I done?" he moaned, running his fingers through his hair as if he'd pull it all out in his anguish. Sinking to the ground, Julien collapsed into soul-shaking sobs.

Mama Nell's mossy eyes opened slowly as the energy from Mother Micheaux washed over her. The priestess watched cautiously from her vantage point still slumped against the hut as Julien's sanity returned and his mother's grip was broken. Her attention darted to Mother Micheaux, who was still trading shots with the unseen force, but understood the message she'd received as strength and consciousness returned. *I've got Solène. Take care of the others.*

Crawling around the heap of blood-stained pins, she ran the back of her hand across her mouth to wipe the blood from her lips. Making her way to the fire, she watched as Zéolie knelt between her brother and her love, taking each of their hands in hers, pushing as much energy as she could spare into them.

"You can't do this yourself, *chérie*. You're gonna need help."

Zéolie looked at her aunt and nodded, without the strength to form the words to answer. Caramel hands covered hers as the priestess spoke, "Camille, she needs you. They all do. Please! We're so close."

Shimmering air, like looking through heat, surrounded them. A silvery mist rolled in like fog, enveloping the four on the ground. Strength poured through their skin at the touch of the cool mist. Power radiated through them from their cores outward.

"What's happening?" Julien asked as he felt his strength being given back to him.

"Camille," Mama Nell answered. "Your grandmother. She's givin' you back what your mother took from you. Your peace and strength. Drink it in, child."

For a moment, Julien did as he was told, closing his eyes and letting the peace pour into his soul. Opening his eyes again, however, his fear returned once more as he saw the battle raging between his mother and Mother Micheaux. "We have to help her. Solène'll kill her."

Zéolie, Louis, and Nell stood as Camille's presence shifted from them to the nun who was weakening under the attack.

"Solène doesn't have a physical body to exhaust, but Mother Micheaux does," Zéolie said. "This has to end."

Mama Nell nodded as the two turned their attention to the warring witches. Hands out, the priestess began to implore the loas for help and protection as Zéolie stepped into the charge, sending a shockwave into the sky that burst in a deafening explosion overhead, drawing her mother's wrath.

"*Damn you*, you little wench!" Solène growled, sending a fireball from the door of the hut. Zéolie deflected it into the tree line before realizing her mistake. The dolls in the trees absorbed the flame and began a chain-reaction, igniting a ring of roaring flame around the clearing. Deep in the forest, the horses shrieked and thrashed, trying to get away from the fire.

Louis' horrified face met Julien's. "In the swamp, the wood was too wet to burn quickly," he yelled over the noise of the flames and popping wood. "It's too dry here!"

Julien nodded and closed his eyes, gathering power in the palms of his hands. A silver flicker danced along his fingertips as his face relaxed. His right hand eased skyward and his fingers flicked toward the smoking canopy. Silver light streamed upwards and vanished into the smoke. Seconds later, amid the thunder and lightning of the battle, rain began to fall. Lightly at first, then in a torrent. Blazing branches hissed as the water doused the flames into steaming coals. Julien held his palm flat, catching the water he'd created. Stunned, he turned to Louis, who smiled at him. "You did it, Julien! You controlled it."

Julien's face softened into a bashful smile. "I had help."

"And you'll have more," Louis answered. "But now, they need you." Julien nodded and stepped forward in line with Mother Micheaux, Mama Nell, and Zéolie, who were trading shots with his mother.

"*No!*" screamed Solène. "Get away from them! You're *mine!*" Her invisible hands clutched at Julien's chest, dragging him by his clothes.

"No, Solène," Julien snarled, digging the heels of his boots into the mud as the rain he had made poured over him.

Mama Nell shouted over the din, "Let him go, Solène! He don't belong to you no more!"

"You filthy whore!" Solène raged. Next to the hut in the mud, the pile of straight pins shuddered then rose into a wall of needles aimed for the priestess. Julien struggled desperately against his mother's grip, unable to help. Zéolie saw the pins glint in the firelight and sent them into the trunks of the surrounding trees, embedding them deep in the charred bark.

Mother Micheaux rained lightning at Solène in the space just in front of a terrified Julien. Shrieking, the witch let him go as he stumbled backwards into the nun. Holding him at arm's length, Mother Micheaux said, "I can't take back what I tried to do to you years ago, and I can't do enough to stop her here."

Julien's eyes filled with tears as the mother superior let her guard down enough for him to see her thoughts. Shaking his dark wet curls violently, he said wide-eyed, "No, you can't do that. Not for me. Zéolie needs you, too!"

His sister's gaze locked on the two of them. "What do you mean? What are you doing?" she asked as panic began to seize her.

Tears mixed with rain streaking down Mother Micheaux's face as she turned her gaze to Zéolie, who rushed to their side. Laying a wrinkled thin hand on the girl's pale cheek, she smiled and nodded. Then, she took that hand and placed it on Julien's forehead. He winced hard as her hand held fast. A sob shook his trembling frame as her other hand rested on his chest, lightly at first, then forcefully. Mama Nell's fingers went to her mouth as words began to flow from the lips of the mother superior. Words Mama Nell knew, but would never utter. Words with more power than any others. Words of self-sacrifice.

The priestess took one of Zéolie's hands in one of her strong ones, and Louis' in the other as she watched the work of the nun. Years washed away from Mother Micheaux's face with the rain. Strength flooded over her as she spoke. Silver mist gathered, taking shape with each word. As the powerful spell was worked, the faint, flowing form of Camille materialized from the mist beside the mother superior, her face filled with love and peace. Over and over, the chant continued as the hands of the nun held Julien fast.

Solène continued to scream and rage around them but could do nothing to penetrate the magnitude of the spell. Lightning flashed and the heatless flame jumped wildly as evidence of her fury but she couldn't touch them.

As the last word rang in the air, Julien's eyes rolled back in his head. Mother Micheaux's form began to shimmer as it continued to hold him upright even in his unconsciousness. With a nod to Camille, her soul separated from her body, taking a step back. The mother superior stood transparent as she watched the shell of her body fall into a heap of black robes at Julien's feet. The boy still stood, unseeing and swaying for a moment.

Mother Micheaux's spirit took one last look at the girl she had traded her soul for and smiled. Tear-filled dark eyes smiled back at her. The nun held her hand out to Camille, who took it in her silver one. Together, they stepped toward Julien as the mother superior's form began to evaporate. Gone were the black robes of her sin. In their place, a pure white mist enveloped Julien's body- Mother

Micheaux's self-sacrifice, giving her own life for the one she once tried to take, transformed into a shield of protection against the vengeful wrath of Julien's mother. Camille turned her silver eyes on her granddaughter and the priestess, smiled once more, and faded into the night.

Julien's body dropped limply next to the body of the mother superior as a vacuum of silence and darkness surrounded the four of them standing in the pitch-black rain.

EPILOGUE

Strange earthy smells surrounded him in the darkness. Smells of herbs and dirt. Voices, muffled and distant, spoke gently. He tried to hear them more clearly, but they seemed to run from him. He wanted to see the owners of the voices, but darkness shrouded them. Then, new sensations. Pain in his limbs. A deep ache in his chest and head. A moan joined the distant voices but seemed closer somehow.

"Julien?" a soft voice said clearly as the moan ceased. "Can you hear me?"

A hand took his, wrapping its fingers around his own. Soft and small. Voices were nearer now, clear. They talked hurriedly and all at once. Excited, but quiet. Willing his eyes to open, the space around him swirled in a wash of muted color before settling into clarity. The light was warm and low, but he could make out a face above him. Auburn waves framing a smile. Somewhere under all the pain in his chest, his heart fluttered as the whispered word formed on his lips.

"Celeste."

The End

COMING SOON

Crescent City Soul
  Book 3 in the Crescent City Series

ACKNOWLEDGMENTS

So many have stood by me offering their support as I walk further along this journey of writing including my amazing family, friends, and publishing team. You know who you are and know how much I value each and every one of you. However, there are a few folks who need a special shout-out.

Laura Kemp, I can't thank you enough for your support, sass, and sense of humor. You keep me sane in the insanity and build me up when I feel deflated. You're amazing!

Carla Vergot, thank you for letting me crash your party! It was a blast and I can't wait to hang out at a blues bar with you again. Thank you for your laughter and friendship!

And, finally, all of the amazing fans, reviewers, book club hosts, and social media group admins who have encouraged this incredible journey. You are the reason I do what I do!

ABOUT THE AUTHOR

Originally from south Louisiana, Nola Nash now makes her home in Brentwood Tennessee, and spends most of her time in Franklin. Growing up in Baton Rouge, she spent long hours onstage or backstage in the local community theaters. Her biggest writing inspiration was the city of New Orleans that gave her at an early age a love of the magic, mystery, and history.

When she isn't writing, Nola is an online high school instructional coach or interviewing authors on Dead Folks Tales and BYOB on Authors on the Air Global Radio Network. She also considers tacos and coffee major food groups.

ALSO BY NOLA NASH

Crescent City Moon

Traveler

House of Mirrors

www.ingramcontent.com/pod-product-compliance
Lightning Source LLC
Chambersburg PA
CBHW061437210726
48287CB00007B/2256